D1287947

Northwater

BY THE SAME AUTHOR:

The Tower of Kilraven

Northwater

BY

CECILY CROWE

Holt, Rinehart and Winston

NEW YORK CHICAGO SAN FRANCISCO

Published simultaneously in Canada by Holt, Rinehart and Winston of Canada, Limited.

Library of Congress Catalog Card Number: 68-12205

PUBLISHED, JULY, 1968
SECOND PRINTING, SEPTEMBER, 1968

Designer: VINCENT TORRE

8688459

Printed in the United States of America

For Paula C. with gratitude

Northwater

I

I came home to Northwater last week.

Poor Kitty; she must have thought the past was behind her forever, and then I had to come back and bring it alive again.

I drove first to their house, hers and her neat little husband's, to get the keys, and I happened upon them out of doors, *en famille*, so to speak, although they are as yet childless. He was on his knees setting out tomato plants, and my sister was in a deck chair wrapped in an old polo coat and was reading aloud to him out of the Sunday *New York Times*. (Has she been improving his mind all these years? He was a garage mechanic when she married him. How like her—resolute and pure in heart!) A charming picture in the cool May sunlight. They live in a little ancient farmhouse, weathered almost black, under a tall, serene elm tree on top of a hill. It was built by Jack's ancestors as I recall from one of Kitty's letters, but it looks as if it had been made for Kitty, to find peace in, safe at last from threats and terror, a refuge.

And at once, before I'd even stopped the car, I felt

I'd broken the spell of a long idyll, and I was an intruder.

And, yes, they both looked up open-mouthed, my sister stunned like the last time I saw her, eleven years ago, as if some terrible blow had befallen her. Oh, they expected me, sooner or later. I had cabled from Zurich, but opening Northwater and getting it ready for me couldn't have been pleasant, and my cable must have reactivated an old nightmare.

It's true, their faces said: she's back.

They had more than one reason for misgivings. I understand the American picture magazines used to carry some rather racy candid shots of me when I was well (well by comparison)—that awful costume party in Venice, for instance, and the rather sad St. Tropez phase. And they know I've been in a sanitarium for a long time but they've never known exactly why, and some of the time neither did I. There were months when I wrote no letters at all, and when I did I told Kitty I'd had a sort of nervous breakdown—anemia, too much high living. . . . The truth but not the whole truth, and not very promising.

I felt their alien virtue in their dread, their resolved stay-at-home normality. I felt prodigal.

But they scrambled to their feet, Jack giving the Ferrari one sweeping expert glance, and I got out and Kitty ran to me and said, "Althea!" and threw her arms around me. This is new, this throwing around of arms. Jack is good for her, as I long ago suspected he would be. (He cultivates her emotions, no doubt, while she cultivates his mind.) I had an impression that he had tucked her up there in her old polo coat on the deck chair near him, settled her in the sun while he worked, got her to read the *Times* to him, because he knew it would soothe her. For there had been the look of the comforted about her, in that first view, and now, close to, I saw that her lids were unnaturally shiny, and I wondered if she'd needed comforting because she'd been crying, although Kitty was never the crying type; tears in her eyes, yes, much more heart-wrenching to the beholder, but even that rarely. Had marriage to Jack helped her to liberate tears as well? And was this crying spell also a result, like reopening a wound, of reopening Northwater?

Then Jack, wiping his hands on his neat behind, came forward too and said to me softly, "Welcome home, Althea," and gave me a firm, calloused, earthy paw. Perhaps a brother-in-lawly kiss will come later. We scarcely knew each other eleven years ago—actually met only once or twice—and for all the twinkle in his eye he is evidently a person of some reserve.

A curious welcome.

They stood side by side with the sun in their eyes, trying to smile, Kate's little heartshaped, heart-wrenching face anxious and pale, and Jack's shoulder just behind hers as if to give her husbandly support. And for a minute or two we didn't know what to say to each other.

A cozy couple, I thought. (Jealously, Althea? Jealously?) I had left for Europe after Mother's death and I had never seen them married. Jack has a hard little body, what Mother would have called a *vulgar* little body (in fact she did call him vulgar, when she was forced to mention him at all), a wiry muscular body, narrow-hipped, large-handed, the kind of body that comes from a long line of gaunt, hard-working, half-starved, independent, blue-eyed Yankees, the ones who settled this part of New England, and I bet he gives Kitty a very good time in bed indeed, and undoubtedly it was this uncorrupted sexuality that Mother meant by vulgar, although she would have been the last to admit or even know it. In fact, wasn't this the main attraction for Kitty in the first place? What less potent life force could have out-rivaled Mother? Poor Kitty, she deserved a little primal fun.

And looking at them, shoulder to shoulder, something twisted in me, knotted like pain, and I tried to keep my smile from sliding into what Dr. Zebstrow called, in German, my "slow sneer of bitterness." The fact is I was glad to see my sister again, glad of *something* for the first time in years, glad almost to the point of a melting, a breaking in myself, too, like tears. There was a sense of safe harbor for me, also, in seeing her again, my little sister. I must have loved her without knowing it, if I was capable of loving anyone. Perhaps this is what I had wanted to come home to.

But I still felt an outsider, excluded, not only by their shoulder-to-shoulder closeness and their tomato patch and their snug little house, but by the look of shock in their eyes, which they were trying hard not to let drain down into their faces. I know I've changed. I've lost a lot of weight, but I had purposely worn my big white coat with the hood, and dark glasses, and, my God, I didn't think I was shocking! But I saw myself as they saw me, and I was aware of things about myself which until then I hadn't given a thought to—the fact that I am now thirty-eight years old, and blonder than I used to be naturally, that my coat and car and jewelry are good but gratingly foreign here—the whole spectacle bizarre, unwholesome, in the strong sunlight of a Sunday afternoon in New England.

And at the same time I remembered myself as they remembered me, eleven years ago, before I went away—lily-like, they used to say, pale and silvery, my long hair streaked by the sun, lids shining from too much sleep rather than tears. And I saw myself as *I* remember myself, dressed in those simple silk frocks that Mother had made for me and that clung to thighs and breasts—nymph-like but numb, in retrospect a gauche creature for all her grace, clumsy within if not without, naïvely corrupt. Did not my doting mother ever see through me?

I pause now in further amazement at myself. It was Dr. Zebstrow who started me on this notebook, because I couldn't remember my dreams, and because, as he said, he wanted me to get into the habit of *thinking*. He said I simply did not *think*. "You are a serious reader, you have a superior vocabulary; why do you not *think?*" And remembering myself as I used to be, here, in summer, I realize I was never concerned with past or future. I was like Daddy, who was an unthinking sort also. Kate looks like him, small and dark, but she was ever a thoughtful soul. (She doesn't take after Mother either, God forbid. Kate was a maverick among us, as if planted there to be our conscience.) At any rate, some maidenhead of mental virginity seems to have broken in me, and now, especially now that I am home—"home"—I expend myself in orgies of self-awareness, wordage, recollections, dissectional cerebration. Hours go by as I lie on the dock in the sun or on my chaise in the gloom, and I do, at last, think! I remember. I weigh. It's Proustian, as if I had all the time in the world and nothing better to do with it.

But as though reading my thoughts, Kitty said in her low voice, so much lower than you would expect in a girl her size, "You still look like a Botticelli." And Jack glanced at her questioningly; she had neglected his art courses.

I'd forgotten how they used to liken me to Botticelli and how it made me slightly sick, because I thought then that Botticelli painted only women of purity. Now, having gazed at some length upon those composed, knowing faces in the Uffizi, I'm not so sure. But it still makes me sick. I said, "I look like an El Greco, darling. Let's not kid ourselves."

Jack's brow wrinkled as if he thought we were exchanging sisterly foreign-language insults, and Kate laughed at me, and then there was a catch in her throat.

She touched my sleeve. (Yes, she touches one now, whereas in the old days she was more apt to stand with her hands clasped behind her back. And I, who never really liked being touched except in the mindlessness of love-making, do not recoil.) "Come in the house," she said. "You must be tired after the long drive."

"No," I told her. "Not this time. I want to get home. I only came for the keys."

And Jack jumped in with, "But, hey, you can't go away like this. You've got to have supper with us. You can't go back to that barn of a place alone!" There is a brightness, a challenge, in his light blue eyes that I rather like, a look that in Europe from one of his class might be considered insolent, but which in America has a brotherly quality, and some nobility; it warms one. It says, You may be an elegant woman, but I am not intimidated because I am a man. Jack comes from a large family, and his sisters and sisters-in-law surely do not go away unfed, unnourished with affection. He can at least offer a woman his masculine shoulders, his home, even the happiness of his satisfied wife.

"I have left a bad-tempered cook scowling on the veranda," I answered, "to say nothing of Bernice, my long-suffering maid. I must get back before the spell of the place turns them to stone."

Kitty went pale again, as if it was not at all hard for her to imagine turning to stone on the veranda of Northwater. And I saw, through her imagination, as it were, the little scene I had just left—the hefty Helga and delicate Bernice standing in the cold shadows made by the great shingled eaves and the stone of the house wall, standing disconsolately in a coldness left over from winter even though the May sun shone elsewhere, left over in fact from the eleven years of desertion; I saw the two black-clad women diminish as I drove off and the dark green peaks and gables take over, soaring into the sky, and these diminishing also in a nest of dark fir trees.

I knew for sure then that Northwater still holds terror for Kitty. She has never got over it.

Jack had run off to fetch the keys, and Kitty, pressing her lips between her teeth, an old mannerism, composed herself, and she assured me she would drop in next day to see if I needed anything, which I did not particularly look forward to her doing, and at last I was able to bid them *au revoir* and get back in my car.

For a moment, while I turned on the ignition and shifted into gear, I studied them again, and they gazed at me. Jack had slipped his arm through Kitty's and they each stood slightly leaning against each other, as couples do when they are seeing someone off, two halves making a whole, and I felt again that acid mixture of envy and irony. "Mr. and Mrs. Jack Gilman," I said, in salute. And they smiled back at me *kindly*.

With relief I left them.

Not to have to talk to anyone, not to have to move, not to have to feel—the complex little cells of emotion shifting within me and with such agonizing effort rearranging themselves! I drove the dozen miles or so from Kitty's house as though on the brink of madness, as though if I delayed another moment the devils would catch up with me and possess me.

And so I came home to Northwater.

I am lying on the dock. A drop of lake water on my eyelid acts as a tiny magnifying glass, and when I look sideways through it I see a gigantic black lash and the deep crevasses of sun-bleached wood. The lake is still ice cold and swimming in it is like shock treatment, but the pure sun bores through me, unties the knots, discoagulates the clotted little cells. The peace of being home, the beloved rest! Yes, beloved, as if I had come home to the arms of a lover after a long, wandering, meaningless journey, such a lover as I never knew, who gives me the tenderness and forgiveness I cannot give myself. "Let nothing disturb thee. . . ." In this peace I am even reminded of lady-saints. . . .

Dr. Robert McCracken Clay has been here. I thought it just as well to establish connections with a local one of his breed. Old Dr. Clay, the town GP who disapproved of me so, with good reason, is long dead, and I was startled to find the name still in the telephone directory. Then I remembered there was a son, red-headed, sober-faced even as a boy, worrying a baseball in a gloved hand, averting his eyes from his father's patients using the side door. He is still red-headed, still sober-faced. He examined me in silence. He resented, perhaps, my making him come to me instead of going to his office. Afterward he gave a short sigh, his lips tightened, and he looked at me reprovingly.

"I'll want to make some tests of course."

"They have all been made," I told him, "in Zurich. There's no doubt about it."

"I shall have to make my own," he said obdurately.

I shrugged. He regarded me for a moment without speaking. He wished, I'm sure, that I were the kind of person to whom he might offer compassion, but I had accepted his initial premise of unfriendliness, and I would have none of his pity. I do not enjoy the disapproval of a person younger than myself, and there is nothing so patronizing as compassion earned by the degree of one's physical impairment. Illness bores me, doctors bore me. They have been cast in the role of God too often. This one with his crinkled carrotty hair and athletic build and his primly idealistic stare must have been idolized by nurses and predicted great things for by senior colleagues. His thigh muscles bulge the trousers of his Dacron suit, and I could picture him in track shorts valiantly running for some cheery university.

Without really thinking I asked, "Why didn't you become a clergyman?" The stern blue presbyterian eyes steadied on me and he answered, "How are your bowels?" which made me laugh. He has no desire to get on a personal footing with me, and this is just as well. The old lust, the old torment, is long dead, and I have no wish to revive it. He wrote out some prescriptions for medications he considered superior to those I'd been given in Zurich, reiterated his insistence on tests at the hospital, and departed.

I am safe. I am home.

It *is* a great barn of a place, and home is a euphemism. In winter when I was a child we lived in Gramercy Park, until Daddy left us, and then after Kitty was born we moved up to a house in the East Sixties, and when this came to seem too impractical we took an apartment on Fifth Avenue overlooking the Metropolitan Museum. But every summer, no matter where we were in winter, we came back to Northwater, which had belonged to Mother's parents. It is the only home I can claim.

Its invisible ghosts don't bother me as they obviously do Kitty. I feel rather tolerant of them, as one does of old family retainers. They are about; one doesn't take them seriously.

Kitty, of course, never knew Daddy. He left before she was born, when I was seven, so actually there is one more ghost for me than for her. But he left his mark on Northwater. Mother's parents, following the heavy-handed architectural fashion of the early 1900's, built a decent, somber, hideous summer mansion; but Daddy brought to it his raciness, his adventurousness, his caprices, his extravagance, his name. ("Rollo North!" they used to say. "Now *there* was a dashing man!")

I see him in the trophies from his wanderings, the mounted heads and fur rugs and Chinese weapons, in the towering stuffed bear at the entrance holding a silver salver for calling cards. (Did any of his girl friends leave ribald notes in the salver as some of my boy friends did?) It was Daddy who designed the candelabra on the newel posts of the great staircase—antlers with an electric light bulb on each prong—and it was he who had the two-story pipe organ installed where the staircase divides to reach the surrounding balconies, so that one feels one is entering the bristling Valhalla of some mad Bavarian prince.

Just a touch of sadism perhaps in the prongs and fangs and swords and spears and slaughtered skins? Is there this streak in all darlings? Perhaps Mother never got rid of any of it for this very reason; its sly cruelty justified her wounded pride.

Ah, yes, Mother's ghost, too. She was a quiet one, almost secretive, as she moved about, except when she was playing the role of Committeewoman, or delivering a manic monologue to me, and it isn't hard to imagine her lingering presence. She wore old-fashioned summer scents, lily of the valley or violet or lavender, and I swear I can smell them still, carried on a vagrant draft, blooming out of the woodwork now that the shutters are open in her long bedroom overlooking the lake, or the adjoining round dressing room. Her chaste white roses still grow in her formal garden, and the wall fountain still drips in the Moorish conservatory where she arranged them. I found her wide-brimmed straw gardening hat hanging there, and her gardening gloves neatly folded in a basket, and just as she left Daddy's mementos to speak for themselves, I simply turned on my heel and walked away from them. Let them hang there until they turn to dust. One can be generous about the mute voices of the dead; she holds no terror for me.

She is gone, and all of her simple, foolish, fanatical life was a prelude to her final tragedy. No, her final death; it doesn't exist for me as a tragedy as it does for Kitty.

Even Kitty's ghost is here, or rather, the ghost of Katherine, as Mother preferred to call her, or Kate, when Mother was in a benevolent mood. (I was the only one who ever called her Kitty, to Mother's disapproval—that faint pinch of the aristocratic nostrils.) Little Katherine, lurking in the shadows, neat in plain linen, not daintily turned out as I was, waiting in the background to be summoned, to be dismissed, sometimes discovered in a reverie, sitting cross-legged in an obscure window seat or a shaded nook of the garden.

But when she was not frightened or flustered or lost in a self-protective dream she could utter low, slow words of wisdom, which had the dismaying effect of putting us in our places, both Mother and me, although Kitty couldn't have known this. It was as if some aged oracle dwelt in her small diffident person. Yes, there was something maddening about her, at times even to me, which made one want to slap her, slam a door on her, crying, "Don't *look* at me like that!"

Well, little Katherine has had the last laugh, hasn't she, Kitty? Mr. and Mrs. Jack Gilman live happily on a hilltop. And even though reopening Northwater has upset her, there is a new life glowing contentedly in her eyes—eleven years of love from Jack, with Jack.

She dropped in the morning after my arrival, as she promised. It was eleven o'clock but I was still asleep. Bernice, who believes in the amenities above all things, however uncharitable her bleak French heart, would not let her leave and insisted on waking me for my sister's first call.

She waited on the screened-in enclosure of the long veranda, among the rattan furniture, and as I came out, lo, there was Katherine again, lost in thought, her hands clasped in her lap, her shoulders slightly hunched. Then she looked up, smiling and straightening her spine, and she became Kitty. A cool gray mist hung over the lawns. I was wearing only a terry cloth robe, but she would not come in out of the damp, and I didn't press her. She wouldn't keep me, she could only stay a moment; she sat with her feet on tiptoe.

Was everything in order, was there anything I needed, was there any errand she could do for me? There was not. Wouldn't I come for supper that night? No. I must have a great taste of peace first, before supper in the snuggery. I told her I was still too tired.

She said, with a little gulp for courage, "Althea, what is it? What is it? You've never really told me. Are you better now? I don't mean to pry, but I must at least know if you're well."

I answered, "I'm much better. I grow stronger every day. You'll see." Well, I *am* better, right now; it's not a lie. And I left it at that.

I'm like a sponge, suddenly, with Kitty. I find myself absorbing every shadow that passes across her face, every flicker of her lashes, as if to make up for the years that I ignored her or tolerated her or at best threw her a fish of affection now and then. For all that there is seemingly an eternity in which to brood, to remember, I feel there is no time to waste in getting to know my sister of the present day. She is not only my link with past and present, she is in some curious way all that I have left of myself. I *need* to know her, to discover what it is in her or of her that brought me close to tears on her hilltop, at first sight of her.

Several times her eyes had moved apprehensively to the open front door. I asked her point blank, "Does Mother still haunt you?"

Her eyes leveled on me, as if my words were going all the way to the back of her head, to the bottom of her soul. People usually look out at one from within the fortress of their personalities, but Kitty, when she gives one all her attention, is all there, mutable, permeable. She pressed her lips together, and then she answered quickly, "Yes, of course." And other thoughts passed across her face, and she seemed to wonder how much she dared confide in me, how close she might come before I shut her out, as I used to.

I could see she was going to fall short and I prompted, "How badly, Kitty? How deeply?"

But she was always one jump ahead of us, and we never knew where her thoughts were leading her. Permeable she might be, but deep within her there was an axis that was herself, an intractable elusive center, and even Mother and her torments couldn't get at it. She made a humorless little smile, and said, "The person I really think about, want to know about, is my father."

Oh, then I felt tired. The yearning for rest clawed at me. "That's easy, Kitty. Some day we'll tuck our feet up and I'll tell you all I remember." I yawned. Now, is this true: that I don't really want to share my memories of Daddy with her?

She gathered herself together, prepared to leave. She was wearing a striped cotton shirtwaist dress and a fawn-colored cardigan, and over her shoulder on a long strap she carried a soft worn pouch of good leather. She looked like a teen-ager, and the purse seemed to possess the keys to her kingdom. It bulged with articles pertaining to her domesticity, her hopes, her youth, her maturity.

She said, "Yes. We have the whole summer. I don't want to weary you, or bore you."

There was no reproach in this, but I smiled. "I used to be so easily bored, didn't I?"

She didn't answer. She was looking upward, and I followed her gaze. She was looking at the dangling oblongs of glass, the wind chimes (Chinese? Japanese?) that someone had thought to restore to their hook in the varnished ceiling—silent now, for there was no breeze.

She said, "I've been coming to this veranda for a long time." It was a confession, I realized, the kind that comes easily at the right moment, when the confessed act finally belongs to the past. "Alone. Even in winter. Perhaps once a month, perhaps not that often. Jack never asked, but he knew. He can tell almost anything I've done or thought just by looking at my face. 'Like an open book,' he says. He understands better than if I tried to explain to him." Katherine again, the very old child, uttering the words in a low prophetic voice.

"And it's odd," she went on, "but I always felt unusually free, free of everything, when I came here. I just stood on this veranda with my back to the house and looked down over the lake and the islands, and because everything was deserted I felt as if I were at the beginning of time, or at the end of it, or both at once. I could feel the way the Indians must have felt when the whole world was anonymous and belonged to them, and I felt that some day perhaps some cataclysm would cause the earth to swallow up the motels and the forests would reclaim the highways and the land would return to its primeval repose, and a few savages would move stealthily under the trees again. I seemed to collect time around me and understand it and yet I stood apart from it, here—here on this veranda! Of all places!" She was half-laughing at herself.

She continued seriously, "Whatever I remembered of this house has been shut up, contained. It was behind me when I stood here, literally behind me, behind the yellowed newspapers pinned inside the windows. But now—" She hesitated.

"Now the house is open again," I murmured.

"Yes. It took Sarah and her helpers two weeks to clean it and get it in order. You remember Sarah Hodge? She used to clean for Mother. She's still going, although her 'Arthur-itis' bothers her."

"Of course I remember Sarah."

"She's going to clean for you regularly, and if you remember Sarah you remember Clarence, her husband. He's done the lawns right along. He'll be coming too.

Well, I trusted Sarah, because I knew you would. I didn't go in to check on things. I even let her put the flowers around." Her hands twisted together. "I still haven't been inside."

I started to speak but she broke in, "It isn't so much that I'm haunted by Mother's—death. It's that I don't know what lies in wait for me in there!" Her hands tore apart and her fingers opened rigidly. "It's as if it's all still there! Her threats, my own guilt—!" Her voice caught and she came to a halt.

I studied her over my folded arms. I was beginning to realize how badly, how deeply, she was affected. And with a curious, compelling morosity, I felt driven to help her. "After eleven years," I said, "you still can't utter the word 'suicide.' "

Her face swung away from me. She stared unseeing over the misted lawns and lake. She said hoarsely, "It was murder, wasn't it?"

I sat paralyzed.

"I mean," she went on, "it was like murder to me. I was involved in it—the scene that preceded it, the threats." She turned to me again, her dark eyes heavy. "I don't think of it as suicide. She murdered herself."

My arms were still folded. Laboriously my heart began to beat again. For a moment a wild, unformed, shattering speculation had obliterated my senses. I breathed again. And then I realized I must take part in Kitty's left-over ordeal.

I stood up. "Come in the house with me now, Kitty.

We must somehow exorcise your devils. Let's get it over with, together."

She glanced up at me gratefully, and she smiled again, and got slowly to her feet also, as one rises from a long and harrowing interview. As I often rose from interviews with Dr. Zebstrow. She said, "Please. Not today." She had spent herself. "Don't worry, I'll do it. Soon. I feel easier about them now—my devils." She gave me a funny, impudent look. (How Jack must love her, with her unpredictability.) "To hell with them," she said. She touched my cheek with a light kiss, natural and fleeting, and hurried down the steps and away across the lawn to her car.

I went inside. No matter how many lights are turned on, even in the daytime, the house is still dark, for the idea behind Northwater's construction was to shut out the summer sun, and it smells stealthily of the Orient and moth balls. "Why do you laugh?" Zebstrow asked, when I described it to him. "There is fear in your eyes."

Oh, my dear gray *Doktor*, we never did get to the bottom of it all, did we? Even Kitty knows there are still unchartered realms in Northwater, precincts of the minds and hearts of its inhabitants, both living and dead, that have never been explored.

And irrevocably she has hung on the air a hideous word: *murder*.

 2 

I called the garage yesterday, and a woman's wheezy voice answered. "Well, I'm sorry, dear," she told me at length, pausing for a harmonic breath, "but I wouldn't be able to tell you about that. I better give you the boss."

After a while the boss said hello, and accustomed to the confusions of European telephone calls I commenced carefully, "This is the Countess Branzini, Mrs. North's daughter. The late Mrs. Rollo North. I am at Northwater for the summer and I'm calling to inquire about Mrs. North's station wagon. I believe it was put in storage after Mrs. North's death. I believe it was stored in your garage."

"That's right, Countess. It was stored here. It still is."

He sounded intimate and amused in contrast to my formality, but I plodded on. "Very well, I would like to have it serviced and put in operating condition and delivered to my residence. It—uh—it will probably need a new battery."

"More than likely." A softness that was not quite a chuckle.

"Who is this?" I demanded. "Do I know you?"

"This is Jack Gilman."

"Jack! I'm sorry. I sounded terribly pompous, didn't I? I've been abroad too long."

"That's all right. How are you?"

"I'm fine, Jack. And you?"

"Just fine. I'll take care of the station wagon. Now, what about your plates?"

"My—?"

"Your plates. Your registration."

"Oh God, yes, I forgot about that."

"Well, you'll have to apply to the town clerk for a permit."

"A permit for what?"

"A permit for a new registration. You fill out an application for the town clerk and you get a permit and then you take it to the state police in the back of the town hall and—"

"Wait a minute. I go to the town clerk and—"

"Get a permit. The town clerk's office, right next to the barber shop."

"The barber shop? What barber shop?"

"Lee Wentworth's barber shop. Listen, Althea, you just ask somebody for the town clerk's office, they'll direct you."

"In Stillbrook?"

"Yes, in Stillbrook: the town clerk of this town. The town of Stillbrook."

"You said the town hall—"

"That's where the state police are. You just ask to be

directed to the town clerk, and you go to her first, and she'll tell you the rest. The town clerk of Stillbrook. Of course, you have to give her the serial number of your car."

"The serial number! Jack, really. All right, how do I—"

"Look, why don't you come straight here first and I'll take you around."

"Maybe I'd better." We laughed. The interchange had brought about something personal between us, supplanting the obliged, second-hand relationship of in-laws. I said, "Are you free now, Jack? I might as well get this over with."

"Come ahead. I'm free."

The town of Stillbrook no longer exists as I once knew it. The days are long gone when Officer Preston, arms authoritatively folded, could lean against the rear fender of a parked car and chat with passers-by, only stepping out into the street now and then to help some Boston dowager back rigidly out of her parking space. There were no motels then, in those prewar days, and only one hotel, a mansarded Civil War relic for traveling salesmen, and a few boarding houses. We were a small set, we summer people; we all knew each other and the townspeople knew us, for many of us had grown up here. Our parents had deliberately chosen a place to summer that wasn't fashionable, but restful and informal, and even though we had our own golf club and tennis courts and spacious houses, we derived a feeling of simplicity from the simplicity of the town, and we felt proprietary about it.

I didn't see a familiar face yesterday, and traffic congests Main Street, and there are parking meters and blinkers and cross-walks and police cruisers, and the elms that shaded the street have been cut down. I miss most of all their shade, or rather, the crystalline fragmented light that fell through their shade, and I miss the morning stillness and fragrance, a fragrance made up of the dew on surrounding lawns and quiet gardens (replaced now with filling stations), and the sparkling lake water of the bay on which the town stands.

Perhaps the time approaches when such things as crystalline air and light and absolute quiet no longer exist, anywhere. Perhaps more of us than Kitty think with subconscious, fateful longing of the cataclysms, erasing our grubby blunders, so that nature may take over and begin again.

"So you're the boss."

"Yes. I'm the boss."

"That's very nice."

"Yes, very nice."

We were still on the half-kidding footing of our telephone conversation, smiling at each other. Jack's office is paneled in imitation knotty pine and furnished with plastic plants, and his secretary, gray-haired and watery-eyed, wheezes companionably over her typewriter in a corner. As I crossed the paved drive-in area for the gasoline pumps, I had heard her, through the open door, admonishing him, "Here she comes. You ought to put your coat on," but he chose to receive me in his shirt-sleeves, looking clean and crisp, as he would receive any of his kinsmen. He was going to be himself with me; perhaps he had stood up to Mother in the same way.

"How is Mrs. Jack Gilman?"

"Mrs. Jack Gilman is fine—"

"You hesitate. Is she really?"

"Yes, I think so. I hope so. Now, about this station wagon. It's hardly been a thousand miles but it's eleven years old. You wouldn't like to turn it in on a new model, would you?" His secretary exhaled a two-toned chord of disapproval. "A nice new country sedan, beautiful this year, I could give you a good trade-in."

"I don't want a country sedan. I want the old station wagon. I'm sentimental about it."

"So am I."

"Oho, you want it yourself. Why?"

"Ask Kate about it sometime."

"You courted her in it," I suggested.

His secretary was goggle-eyed. He said, "Let's go have a look at it."

He opened the door into a cavernous garage-din—accelerated engines and unexplained crashes; garage-eyes, brief and blank, looked up at me, picking my way after the boss. "Calvin!" he called, and an elderly unwrinkled man dropped a spanner on the concrete floor without change of expression and followed us into a shed at the rear. It must once have been a livery stable; it smelled still of horses, and a fine hay-dust had filtered down over everything, a Ford sedan of the late thirties and a high old Franklin with cut glass vases over the back seat, and Mother's station wagon.

"What a fire trap," said Jack. "We ought to pull this shed down."

"Be here fifty years from now," said Calvin pessimistically.

"Countess Branzini wants her mother's station wagon, this here. Let's get this tarpaulin off, look it over."

Calvin got the tarpaulin off and they looked it over, communing in the manner of men with motors, as if I weren't there.

"How soon can you get it ready?"

"Depends. Mebbe the tires ain't held up."

"You get it ready, and I'll take it out to her."

"No plates."

"It's got the old ones on, green on white, same as now. A mile down the lake road, who would notice?"

Calvin stared at Jack with disbelief. "Ayah."

"You just get it ready, Calvin, then look the other way."

Calvin took off his cap and hurled it to the floor. "Darn it, she's going to git new plates, ain't she? You can wait 'til she gits the new ones on, can't you? Ain't you never going to grow up?"

Jack folded his arms, laughing softly, egging him on.

Calvin stooped and picked up his cap and settled it again on his head. "Terrible kidder, you are. Don't know why I *evah* take you seriously. Kinda thing you *woulda* done, back-along."

"You never did learn to respect me, that's your trouble." Jack's hand rested for a moment on Calvin's shoulder. "Tried to talk her into a trade-in. No dice."

"Eight hundred seventy-two miles," said Calvin, reading the speedometer. "Practically brand new."

"Be here fifty years from now."

"Ayah." Calvin nodded composedly. "Now you take Rollo North."

Suddenly I existed again, and Jack was my brother-in-law. "Yes," he said. "This lady's father. What about him?"

"Rollo North," Calvin repeated softly, knowing he had our attention but ignoring us; Rollo North had left something of himself with Calvin that he couldn't possibly have left with anyone else. "Never had the same ca' two years running. I bet you I could remember every ca' that man ever owned if I was t'set down to it. Had a Stutz, is the first one I recall, and then Packards several years, and one a them special Chrysler roadsters with the windows in the deck of the rumble seat, and a Cord convertible, front-wheel drive, yellow. Took a bunch of young folk up Mount Washington, all had to git out and walk the last mile, weight went onto her rear wheels and she wouldn't pull 'em up. Turned to Cadillacs finally, even had one a them sixteen-cylinder models, didn't last long, big as a hearse and burned up more gas than a fire engine. I tell you, he knew his ca's, and he took good care of 'em, wouldn't let nobody touch 'em 'cept me. Took the kids for rides, too, clear out to Greenvale and back. Weren't no ca's like that *around* here in the old days, and they used to congregate in front of the bank and wait for him, and he would say, 'Pile in,' and off they would go. All got ca' sick once, too, one sta'ted it and the others followed, even one old coon dog who happened to go along. What a mess. Turned that one right in. Ayah, Rollo North. Knew his ca's. Enjoyed 'em. Never knew what he was going to turn up with next."

Rollo North all over, I thought. Jack gave an odd little sigh. He said, "Well, let's get the serial number."

Emerging from the shed he turned to me, "Want to run me up to the town clerk's office? I'd like a ride in that Ferrari. And I don't get car sick."

"You can drive it if you want to."

"That's what I hoped you'd say."

"What did you mean, Jack, you hoped Kate was well?" We had finished the rigmarole of getting license plates and I'd accepted his invitation to a cup of coffee in the local diner.

"She's a little shook up, that's all. Memories."

"Will she get over it?"

"Of course she'll get over it." Something about his lowered lids told me this was his province; he would just as soon not go into it with me. Then he looked up, and I was struck by his extraordinary long-lashed eyes, their lightness, pale blue or green or gray—a color between all three; they seemed to encompass everything, missed nothing. All the time we sat there, people passing in and out spoke to him, and he answered, "Hi, Joe. Hi, Harold," without turning, as if he could see through the back of his head. He said to me, "She got over a lot worse than this." His lids shut me out again.

Did she? Did she entirely? I said, "Does anything shake *you* up?"

He gave a breath of a laugh. "You'd be surprised."

"Kate, for instance."

The silvery bright eyes rested on me seriously a second, saying, I don't kid about this. "Yes, Kate."

"Tell me about the station wagon."

"I brought it out to Northwater when it was new. I was a mechanic then. I serviced it and delivered it."

"And that's when you met Kate?"

"That's when I met Kate."

"Mother wasn't around? I wasn't around?"

"Nobody was around. Only Kate."

"And that's when you first set eyes on her."

"Oh no. I grew up in this town, remember, and you have been summering here since you were children, and I always had eyes."

"For Kate?"

"For Kate." Yes, he was telling me, you were the glamour girl, but it was Kate who shook me up. Why? I wanted to know these things. I wanted to know what he had seen in Kate from the start, what she had seen in him; I wanted to know him as Kate's husband. I said, "Why should I remember you grew up in this town?"

"Because I met you once, years ago, when I was a kid. I was working behind the counter at Austin's, that place where you all used to eat after the Saturday night club dances. Though I don't suppose there's any reason why you should remember. Murph introduced us."

"Murph." I sat back, away from my cup. "Oh."

"Well, that was a long time ago. I better get back on the job. I'll take care of the station wagon, and it was nice talking to you."

"Yes. It was nice talking to you." We left the booth.

"You have a standing invitation to our house, you know."

"Yes. Thank you. I'll take you up on it. Soon. I've needed a little time to get my bearings."

"We understand that." We were standing out in the sunlight. "Look," he said. A little crowd had gathered around the Ferrari. "Like father like daughter."

"Too true."

"Well, good-by, Althea."

"Good-by." And we parted on a flat, distant note after all. I had come too close to teasing him about Kate, and he wouldn't stand for that. Maybe he threw in the name of Murph to shake *me* up.

The boathouse is to the right of me as I lie here on the dock. It matches the house with its overhanging eaves and diamond-paned windows. Upstairs at the back there is a storage room for boat cushions and paddles and so on, and next to it a john, and at the front over the water there is a large echoing varnished room with a Ping-pong table and other games where we played on rainy days when we were children. It also has two lounges that could be made up into beds for an overflow of guests, especially the youths Mother considered too boisterous for the house.

At least, I suppose it's all there as it used to be. Like Kate and the main house, I can't bring myself to go upstairs in the boathouse. Murph and I used it. How old was I then, fourteen? Fifteen?

"Murph was the first one?" Zebstrow dangled his gold watch from a chain as he usually did when the hour was drawing to a close.

"Yes."

"Tell me about it. How did it happen?"

"He worked at an eating place we used to go to after dances. He was a great handsome fellow, one of those black Irish with black eyes. He came from what you might call the slums of Stillbrook, a street where people put old washing machines and prolapsed sofas on their porches, and there was always a broken-down car or two in the backyard. We looked each other over for a long time. I was a virgin and I was longing not to be one." I minded telling Zebstrow about this. I spoke matter-of-factly, trying not to give it undue importance, but I realized from the quivery stirring in me that it was more important than I had ever believed. "I made a date with him to row over to Northwater, late at night. I took him up to the playroom in the boathouse. He came over almost every night that summer."

"Were you in love with him?"

"I was in love with the way he made me feel."

"And that was—?"

"Glad. Glad!" I didn't want to go on, but the words pushed out. "And sad, too, sometimes. Very sad."

"Why did you not choose someone of your own background?"

"Oh, you don't know what those Groton, St. Paul's types were like—wary, leering, gossipy, overbred. Their idea of a big time was a scramble in the back of a car."

"And yet you eloped with one."

"But that was long after Murph! All my friends were getting married by then, and Mother had started delivering monologues about my wedding, even though I wasn't engaged to anyone. It was going to put everyone in his place, of course; it was going to be the biggest, goddamnedest wedding the countryside had ever seen."

"And you wanted to cheat her out of it?"

I shook my head in confusion; I pressed my damp fists together in my lap. "It wasn't only that. I got the idea into my head that marriage might solve everything. I thought something might work!" I was suddenly silent, and Zebstrow, eyes watchful, waited for more, compelled more. I blurted out, "Or maybe I knew it wouldn't work all along! Within a year I was back at Northwater as if nothing had happened."

"Maybe," Zebstrow suggested, "you didn't want it to work."

"I don't know, I don't know!"

"Maybe you were taking something out on this Groton, St. Paul's man."

"I don't know!"

"And then Branzini," he murmured, "who was evidently the last word in overbreeding."

"Why," I wailed, "do we have to go over and over these things?"

But a kind of Zebstrow-induced surrender was quieting me, as it usually did toward the end of the interview, and when he didn't answer I went on with a sigh, "Perhaps the full-bloodedness had gone out of me, too, by that time. I had left the States after a family tragedy, burned my bridges; I came to Europe to lose myself. I was actually in search of some all-purpose, all-absorbing masquerade. I wanted to be—someone else."

"And were you?"

"Yes!" I challenged him. "Yes, I was!"

"All right." He didn't pursue the point. "Let us get back to this gladness, this sadness, with Murph."

At once I turned balky again. "Let us not! Dear *Doktor*, why dwell on it? It was only an episode, the first one to be sure, and I learned from it, but it certainly wasn't the last. I didn't cry when I said good-by to Murph. It was long before that, in the middle of the summer, the first time I ever really cried, when I knew I *would* eventually say good-by to him and it would all come to mean nothing—" My voice broke and I couldn't go on.

After a moment Zebstrow glanced at his watch and pocketed it. The hour was at an end. "And did it?" he asked absently. "Did it come to mean nothing?" Without waiting for an answer he rose to shake my hand and bow me out.

I put down my pen now for another shock treatment in the lake. I swim with my eyes open in a pale green and sand-colored limbo, and when I emerge I am sobbing with the cold, but the clutching in my breast has let go. I am awake in the present again. The patients in the sanitarium, after the real shock treatment, held their heads in their hands and tried to remember their own names. "Excuse me, did I tell you my name? Did I tell you if I had a husband?"

Yes, better not to dwell on Murph, better to stay out of the boathouse. I took others up there, of course, in the years that followed, but they were none of them Murph, and yet in a sense they were all Murph. Perhaps, as terror still exists for Kate in the main house, passion still exists for me in the boathouse, and if I were to open the door the white-hotness might explode in my face, filling my mouth and eyes with ashes, and in the fraction of a second I could become a starved, a starving, woman.

An old question arises: what did Mother know of Murph? What did she know of all the others? Old Dr. Clay *must* have told her something. Why could she look the other way for me as she hadn't been able to do for Daddy? Her eyes glittered for me, watching me from the sidelines at club dances. She must have known that everyone in the row of elders despised me, and yet she wore a little smile of triumph!

Kitty, unlike me, was straightforward. We were finishing dinner, and she announced softly during a silence, "I am going out. I have a date with Jack Gilman."

Mother's mouth hung open. She said mechanically,

still unable to believe her ears, "I forbid it!" Kitty stared back at her. Mother commenced to mobilize her forces. And I saw destruction begin at that moment. I saw the determination to annihilate rise with the vertical shine of knives in Mother's eyes. "That vulgar boy who works in the *garage?*" Her voice rose shrilly. "I absolutely forbid it!"

And a familiar coolness came down over me. I smiled. I was used to seeing Kitty crushed, and out of the spasm of coolness there seemed to come once more, distilled, one small drop of acid that fell into a reservoir, an acid reservoir like a deep cobalt-colored pool in a subterranean cave. . . .

But Mother had struck that bedrock in Kitty. There was an opaqueness in Kitty's eyes. They rested on Mother distantly. Not a muscle of her face changed. I held my breath. The candle flames quivered.

Kitty said, "I'm sorry. I'm going." And she rose and quietly left the room. Her one romance. Her one love.

I had to laugh at Mother's expression. Her irresistible force had met an immovable object. She picked up her goblet and hurled water in my face, and I laughed all the harder.

Oh, Zebstrow, I sigh again, was it to piece these memories together that I learned to think? Was that, in fact, your intention?

3

Resignedly I went up to the hospital for the tests Rob Clay had insisted on. He had made the appointment for me, but when I chanced to pass him in the corridor, deep in talk with another white-coated staff member, he glanced at me as if he wondered what I was doing there. How these people do render one, however inadvertently, soulless, sexless, and superfluous. I moved on, grasping my little white card, to the laboratory.

Discouraged, depersonalized, I emerged from the hospital and stood at loose ends on the steps for a moment, gazing at Main Street as it goes up the hill out of Stillbrook. On the crest, over the golf course, there is a new Catholic church of modern design, and I went to my car and drove up to it. Not to pray, or to redeem my soul, for hypocrisy at least is not one of my traits, but more in the manner of a tourist in Europe who looks at architecture and rests his feet at the same time.

St. Michael's. All roof and glass, it floats in its own park, with an unbroken view of greens, woods, and lake. What would it be like inside—the usual varnished oak and bleeding statues? But as I sat down in the back of the empty nave I realized I had come upon a genuine masterwork, all of a piece with its quiet weight and light, giving me that sudden delighted sense of an unfamiliar dimension. The roof soars into shadows, its massive structural beams field-gray like wintered grass, and a great bronze crucifix seems suspended in midair. Gray-brown, solid, serene, the interior includes the exterior, the surrounding sweep of landscape, through its transparent walls. No gilt, no wax flowers; only the floating cross, and beneath it the sanctuary candle glowing mysteriously as though breathing, whispering.

I sat there for a while in an agreeable state of consent, liberated, detached from myself, sickly fatigue snuffed out by the sheer weight of silence and simplicity.

But it was Quaker-silent, this gray simplicity, with the compelling urge toward utterance, and I was aware of my ears ringing. I felt then an acutely uncomfortable pressure bearing down on me, to the point of suffocation, and, terrified, like a fish out of water, I got up to leave.

I had dropped some coins in a box at the door when a priest came forward, in the manner of priests, out of nowhere. Slight in build, graying, somewhat unshaven, he said good morning and thanked me with a French accent, and quieting, I told him I thought the church very lovely.

"Oh yes," he agreed, glancing about him in a pleased way, hands loosely clasped together, as though nothing that was lovely surprised him, and he went on in his charming accent, "It is what a church should be, isn't it, not a place to be sad or afraid but to be *tranquil*." He gave the word the French pronunciation.

I couldn't answer that truthfully. I looked back at the radiant view. "What is it like when the sun isn't shining?"

"Oh, then it is even more lovely. You must come and see." He seemed to move lightly all the time he spoke, as if he weren't quite firmly rooted to the ground, and his steel-rimmed spectacles caught reflections as he turned his head, and a silver tooth gleamed. His collar didn't fit his neck snugly. He seemed more young than old, but his age, like that of creatures whose life span is not related to ours, was impossible to guess.

"In November, for instance," he continued, "when everything is—*grave*," again the French pronunciation, so much more evocative than the English, "and you can see the stone walls and the shape of the trees. Then the church is very beautiful, very still and beautiful."

"Who designed it, Father?"

"Men," he answered vaguely, smiling and spreading his hands in wonder. "Artists. It was a great battle at times, everyone wanted a hand in it, and we had to be like i-ron—i-ron?—not to accept gifts of stained glass and other decorations. No, I said, let us wait and see what they make. Do you summer here? Have we met before?" (" 'ave we met *be*-fore?")

I said we had not and we introduced ourselves and briefly touched hands. He is Father Bonneau and comes from Quebec.

I have known any number of priests. One cannot live in Rome for a time and not do so: fat ones and emaciated ones, garrulous and taciturn, intelligent and dull, sleek and ascetic, jolly and forbidding. Branzini had his devout moments, which, however perfunctory, he took quite seriously.

But as I chatted with this Father Bonneau another storm began to possess me. He kept shifting about lightly, glancing hither and yon and smiling, and I found myself longing like a child to restrain him, capture him for an instant, take from him whatever it was that pleased him and made him so elusive, both gentle and invulnerable, innocent and worldly, so gracefully at ease in his shabbiness, obliterating personality and releasing spirit. Stubbornly I refused to think the obvious thing: *God*. It mustn't be as difficult as that! A terrible need burned in me, an aggressive demand very close to rage.

I heard myself saying somberly, "I am not a Catholic or a church-goer."

"But you are welcome," he told me without hesitation. "Come and sit any time!"

I knew I mustn't go on standing there, staring at him, my teeth clenched. In the next instant I might cry out, "Father!" and go down on my knees to him. But I couldn't face the desolation of leaving him, letting go of him. He must give me *some*thing! He must come out of his charmed isolation and meet me on some common ground, he must come out of his spiritual world to my earthly one, for a moment, for a moment only, and extricate me, release me! All of my frivolous, leaden days hung upon me like a curtain and he must see through them to me, to whatever there was of me that *he* could see.

"I am dying," I told him. "I have come home to die."

He turned to me slowly, and rather than diminish and evaporate, his joy, his innocence, seemed to increase, to shower over me. And yet in that instant he was much the more solid of the two of us, at least the more total, for I was now in fragments; multicolored sections of myself, I felt, joggled kaleidoscopically before his eyes, and I no longer knew myself. Not even in the days of drug-taking had I felt so disintegrated.

But dying to Father Bonneau was not what it was to me, just as living was not earth-bound. The little smile never left his face. He said softly, "Then you must make peace with yourself."

"Yes," I said. I exhaled deeply in a sigh. "Yes."

Suddenly I wanted to laugh. No buck-up-old-girl talk, no surely not, no exhortation, not even the word "God." He couldn't have put it more simply or said anything more sensible. "Thank you, Father. You've told me what I needed to hear."

"You knew it already," he chided gently.

I realized he was not moving about just now, which perhaps made him seem so much more solid, and his stillness was in itself a kind of blessing. Slowly, dazed, I pulled the ceremonial scarf from my head, and he opened the outer door for me.

"Come back," he told me, nodding as if I had already agreed to do so.

I smiled and didn't answer, and went down the walk. Colorlessly, the joints indistinct, the fragments had come together again, and for better or worse, pale and spent, I was whole again.

Kitty, I thought, reaching my car; I must begin with Kitty. I sat motionless for a moment. What was it she wanted to know? How much is good for her to know?

A sudden memory, a picture, flashing irrelevantly out of the labyrinth of my mind like the sea casting up a bit of treasure.

The Umbrian hills, somewhere on the road north from Rome. Branzini and I are on our way to the villa in Tuscany, being driven in the old Rolls at the mad, fanfared pace of Italian chauffeurs. One gets used to it. I relax and let Giulio decide whether we're going to kill an old lady crossing the street or two men on a scooter; miraculously, with split-second timing, they make room for us. It is Sunday, noon. The bells in the hill towns cease ringing and the processions of black-garbed church-goers thin out. The country grows richer in vineyards and orchards, the colors darker, the air more luminous.

Branzini and I are silent. We have been to a late party the night before and are more than usually numbed, shrunk within ourselves. The abyss between two people, side by side—there is no loneliness like it. His profile on my left is handsomely brooding, the black brows cloaking a disillusionment more hereditary than environmental, as if the centuries had gradually withdrawn the genes of joy from the family, replacing them all the more perniciously with intelligence, beauty of face and body, indifference to good and evil.

And then suddenly the tableau on our right, a fleeting picture as we speed by: a peasant family seated around a table under their grape arbor, and on the table two bottles of wine and one beautiful pink watermelon cut in half. That is all. No one moves. They sit in patient Sunday repose, their care-worn hands at rest in their laps.

They are gone in an instant. But I come to, out of my deadly apathy; some little light goes on within me. Not only because it was a Renaissance miniature, with its somber blues and greens, its wines and fruit and reverent quiescence, not only because I recognize it as a scene that imprints itself on the mind forever; I have glimpsed something even more meaningful.

I turn in wonder to Branzini. He has seen it, too; his eyes, faintly derisive, meet mine, asking, What did you make of it?

I say, my voice thinned, "They were in a state of grace, weren't they?"

He smiles with an elongation of his black-lashed lids. He answers, "How would you know that?"

Rebuffed, I turn away. His tiny civilized cruelties haven't penetrated my shell in a long time, but now an extraordinary blush rises in my cheeks.

After a moment he breathes, "You surprise me." Does he mean the blush, or the presumptuous remark about grace? "You still have the ability to surprise me." He takes my hand, caresses my arm. He places my hand in his lap. He wants me; after months of disinterest, he wants me. He raps on the glass and Giulio gaily drives with his eyes on his master and the back of his head to the road. "We will stop at the inn in Todi," Branzini tells him.

And the tableau, the family under the grape arbor with the pink watermelon, which I thought so unforgettable, leaves my mind completely.

Until now. Why has it waited until this moment? Why should Father Bonneau have brought it back to me?

My voice on the telephone must have demonstrated my return more vividly than my actual appearance. I heard a little gasp before Kitty cried, "Althea!" There was delight, almost relief, in her voice; perhaps my reality begins to counteract her phantoms.

I asked if I might come to see her that afternoon.

Oh dear, she said, she was doing some last-minute cooking. She was having friends for dinner that night, just two couples, but one of them was the gourmet sort, that's why she was taking special pains. But they were close friends and it was really going to be quite informal, and wouldn't I join them?

The words were gathered on my tongue to refuse. I couldn't make the effort to meet strangers. I was already depleted by the visit to the hospital and the encounter with Father Bonneau. And I confess, I was a little put out that Kitty wouldn't drop everything and see me that afternoon, my first offer to come to her; an old bitchy feeling, the imperiousness of the invalid.

But it intrigued me, Kitty's social life, and I was curious about her friends. I forget sometimes here in Northwater that she is Kitty and no longer Mother's Katherine, the Katherine who sat so unobtrusively at little gatherings on the veranda under the tinkling oblongs of glass, ready to rise in an instant when an older woman rose, or to pass cups and tea cakes, her face a perfect blank and yet so cognizant of what was going on around her that her ready good manners must have been almost as disconcerting as my bad ones. I was even curious about her ability to cook. I have to reassure myself of her metamorphosis, I am almost jealous of it, I don't want her to get away with any accomplishment without my knowing about it and crediting her with it.

I remembered Father Bonneau's parting words, and I said, "If you don't mind an extra woman—"

Again her voice burst over the wire. "Oh, you'll come! You're *not* an extra woman, Althea, you're my glamorous sister and it will be lovely to show you off. I didn't think you'd let me. Of course I wanted it to be just the three of us at first, you and Jack and I, so we could get to know each other, but we can always do that. It's going to be a buffet, and you'll like the Goodfellows, and the Clays—you remember old Dr. Clay, this is his son—and we'll arrange the threesome another time—"

Her warm candid babble pleased me, and I wondered,

Is this how it should be between sisters? This anticipation, this sense of good news, a feeling that anything she says, however trivial, is more important to me than anything anyone else says? There was never any intimacy between us or any rivalry, for my supremacy was always taken for granted; we had been separated all our lives, we had always been strangers. This, I thought, this give and take of identity, even over the telephone, must be the essence of sisterhood. I am learning some of the fundamentals of life, belatedly, from Kitty.

"Jack will be glad, too!" she said.

I sat by the phone after we'd hung up, smiling at myself, feeling like a postdebutante. It had been so long since I had "gone out." Yes, there was Jack, too, I must never forget that: the quiet force in the background, the poor man's Pygmalion, the catalyst. Were these his friends as well? Would Kitty permit herself to entertain people who were out of his depth? The word "gourmet" struck a contrary note. Surely that wouldn't be the dour Robert McCracken Clay? And what sort of woman would *he* surrender himself to?

I must see for myself.

They greeted me on the granite step outside the kitchen door and took me in, and Kitty's refuge materialized.

"This is Jack's creation," she began proudly. "He installed everything himself!" It was a dazzling little clinic of copper equipment and shining gadgets, glowing concealed lights, wall ovens, push buttons, the kind of kitchen that would make the one in Branzini's Tuscan villa (I never even set eyes on the one in Rome) look like the cave of primitive man. The makings of supper were neatly organized on gleaming counters, and there was a fragrance of herbs and wine.

"Jack of all trades," he murmured deprecatingly. He was freshly bathed and shaved and he had had what Mother would have called a vulgar haircut and his ears stuck out, but he was attractive in a blue jacket, and Kitty looked charming in pink linen. If she were still harrowed by the reopening of Northwater she didn't show it tonight, and once again my eyes fastened covetously, thankfully, on the established contentment in her face.

"Now we go into Kitty's domain," he said, leading the way to a tiny parlor.

She had used red velvet for fabric. Old wood gleamed and brass shone, and there were pewter mugs and luster pitchers of late spring flowers tucked in dark corners. I could see it cozily reflecting the firelight while the snows of winter swarmed outside, or cool and shadowed in the heat of summer, and my thankful envy began to fill me with a curious queasiness. This house of love and self-sufficiency was a little more than I could stomach. ("*I all alone beweep my outcast state. . . .*")

"Any time you feel like getting back to the womb," said Kitty, as if reading my thoughts, "come and curl up here."

"It looks like you, Kitty."

She smiled, a little ruefully. "It looks like what most

people think of as me." Her flat tone startled me. Then she laughed. "You should hear Jack go on about it!"

"Well, but good Lord," he responded, half-seriously, "look again, Althea. You can hardly see out the windows, these little hand-blown panes. I said let me put in a picture window at least, there's a beautiful view out there, but Kate nearly fell apart at the idea. And nothing is plumb, she wouldn't even let me refloor it, and no damper will fit this old chimney," he swung a foot at the small faded bricks, "so it sucks up the heat—"

"You see?" Kate exulted. "He loves it! It was built by his own forebears. He just talks like this because he loves it."

"She'll get tired of it," Jack sang on softly, "she'll get fed up with the inconvenience, way out in the middle of nowhere, and we'll sell it to some city guy who thinks he wants to live close to Nature, and I'll build her a *real* house nearer town, not in a class with Northwater of course, but—"

"A split-level-rambler-ranch-type!" Kitty laughed. It was a duet—Jack covering his pride, his uncertainty that it was good enough for her, and Kate reassuring him with laughter.

They showed me a pretty guest room, with another fireplace opening from the central chimney, and an ultra-modern bath, also installed by Jack, and their own bedroom, largely occupied by their—of course—double bed, and lastly, coming round full circle, the "borning room" off the kitchen, which Kitty used for sewing and laundry.

They felt something about this room that they couldn't tell me; there was a tight little silence between them as they gazed at it, and Kitty's fingers were stiffly interlaced. The nursery-to-be, I guessed, for the hoped-for child. Kitty was thirty now, nearly thirty-one. My eyes quickly passed over her face and I saw that it was inconsolable.

So there was a flaw in their idyll after all, even apart from Northwater. The spark of an old half-remembered anger flared in me, as if I too were frustrated. I couldn't tolerate Kitty's looking like that, her having to want so deeply for anything! Not now, when she had her refuge, her Jack, and a nearly perfect contentment.

But Jack's hand had moved to her arm. "We better get back to the Goodfellows," he said softly.

"Yes." She roused herself. "Oh, yes. Goodness, I almost forgot about them!"

We traversed the parlor again and came out on a little grass terrace overlooking the view of lake and hills, and I was introduced to Simon and Margo Goodfellow, a couple whose outlandishness I wasn't prepared for, not in friends of Kitty and Jack; the gourmets, without doubt. Then everyone was at once involved in settling on something to drink, and I said as usual, "Nothing thanks," for I never could handle more than a sip of wine, but when I was seated Jack bent over me and asked, "Would you like some iced coffee with me? I made it, it was such a warm evening," and I told him it sounded delicious.

I am touched when a devoted husband's awareness

includes other women besides his wife, and he takes them under the same wing; perhaps it's a measure of his devotion. I grow fond of this man, Kitty's husband, which surprises me, as I hadn't expected to form an independent feeling for him apart from her. For all that he is a tease, playing an odd game of modest self-mockery, there is something like Kitty's core of truth in him, an unshakable faith of some kind, in himself, in mankind perhaps, in a way of life opposed to self-interest. I don't know if I shall get to know him well, or if he will get to know me, apart from Kitty, but even this arm's length in-law relationship is interesting, and new to me, with its element of mutual respect, and it strangely comforts me.

He disappeared to make the drinks, and Kitty excused herself a few moments later to look after dinner, and the Goodfellows and I were free to turn our full attention upon each other, trying not to be too obviously agog—they no doubt for the prodigal sister, the slightly *déclassée* contessa, and I for the red-headed Margo in a shocking pink Mexican dress and the buck-toothed, stork-like Simon.

Perhaps he represents the new Groton, St. Paul's type. In my day they were shorter and stockier and they drank harder and dutifully set about making money, but this generation seems to go in for sober eggheadism—buying a country newspaper, for instance, as Simon has done, and entering local politics. He wears old-fashioned gold-rimmed spectacles, perfectly round, leaves off his r's and speaks with a slight, well-bred lisp, and his Brooks Brothers suit needs pressing. He seems to ponder, as he stares at one, the moot double-question: how does she stack up against my acquired antisnob standards, and how does she stack up against the snob-ones of my upbringing?

He was having a difficult time of it, with me, a titled American not given to small talk, and he began, "So you are the owner of the famous white Ferrari. You have the town of Stillbrook absolutely *bouleversé*, you know," and I answered with a shrug, "Oh, *merde*." He stared at me nonplussed and a peal of laughter like ripe fruit came from his wife.

Flaming-haired, bell-voiced, overly made up and perfumed, she is like a Toulouse-Lautrec caricature. She out-bohemians Bohemia. Yet she too went to Chapin, it somehow came out, reads French novels in French and Italian poetry in Italian. She is a flamboyant being who can afford to kick over the traces of genteel upbringing not because she never actually had one but because she can never actually get rid of it.

In this setting we were predisposed to like each other. A scent of old pastures, growing stronger as twilight approached, encircled us, and the late sunlight sent a long caressing light over the landscape spread out below; the lake lay vibrating, sheen-enameled, indigo, and the islands and ranks of distant hills hovered in pearly space. Perhaps we recognized in each other something of that same outcasthood, people who could no longer claim any particular society, who would never find a cozy refuge. Kitty's and Jack's aura held us captive and rendered us charitable.

Having seen me safely through my first unflinching impression of himself, Simon felt free to subside into quietness, only venturing a quip now and then with Jack, whom he holds in open esteem and affection, or supplying some bit of erudite information when the rest of the company was stymied. In twenty years, I mused, he would be an old sage, stoop-shouldered and crotchety.

Or would his wife, if she stuck with him, keep him mellow? Her rich laugh pealed out continually, summoning us like a call to conviviality, rousing us from separate dreams: we are together, this is the only hour that counts! She was like some Epicurean incarnation in our midst, bent not so much on enjoying herself as on our enjoying ourselves with her.

Jack had sat down beside me, his elbows on the arms of his camp stool, his large hands dangling, his thin knees apart, and his feet curled inward, but not awkwardly; on the contrary, he was cat-like, poised to move, not a thread of tension tugging at him anywhere. He was watchful, wearing his mysterious little smile, which might have meant he had never really taken for granted his being in this kind of company, or that he enjoyed it twice as much as we did. He anticipated our needs, rising unobtrusively to produce a second round of drinks, light a cigarette, or assist Kitty behind the scenes.

She too returned, and this is the social Kitty I came to see. Her small body is animated, as it never was on the veranda of Northwater, and half her mind is on her kitchen. Yet a radiance fills her face, she looks across at me and smiles, laughs at Margo, glances confidently at Jack. Her face with its dark mobile eyebrows mirrors everything that is said, every mood that passes over us. I think Simon, who doesn't look at her very often, is afraid of falling in love with her. A fervent gladness seems to press behind her face, her eyes, as if she is only once removed from tears; gladness to have me here, to have us all here, to share the view she takes in wordlessly again and again.

And yet this is the girl who planted a terrible word in my mind.

I think to myself how she was conceived in a moment of forgiveness or fury, before Daddy left us for good. Was it this conception that tempered her, made her different from us, gave her this nearness to anguish? I don't think it was alone her fatherlessness, or the dreadfulness of life with Mother, her girlhood as handmaiden, her education in self-effacement—and, I realize, self-defense. She must have been different before she was born. Perhaps her violent prenatal baptism set a mark on her, when Mother, deserted and pregnant, threw herself into the lake with a loud splash in the middle of the night and was ignominiously rescued by Clarence Hodge, the gardener.

And I ask myself, not for the first time: was this small, quiet, deep-eyed girl capable of violence, too?

The Clays arrived. The muscular fair-haired doctor shook hands reservedly and forbearingly, somewhat like the President of the United States who has just come from a tremendous hand-shaking reception, and then he sat down and crossed his knees and composed himself judiciously to listen to the light-hearted conversation around him.

Mrs. Clay is an All-American girl; I might have known —beyond reproach, collected, competitive, tanned and sturdy, a healthy flush in her cheeks, shining brown hair. She gave me one rather intimidated glance and from then on talked over and around me. In an authoritative voice, just a shade too loud, she began to explain their lateness, not, apparently, due so much to her husband's emergency call as to her own last-minute organization of their seven children; each one, by nickname (Taddie, Josh, Priss—), was about to be accounted for, but Margo had had two or three drinks by now and expertly cut her off, laughing inappropriately, and ran off with the conversation herself.

Mrs. Clay resorted to drawing up a chair by Simon and telling him something long and important in an exclusive undertone, to which he was evidently forced to respond uncomfortably in an old pre-antisnob manner. To my surprise it was Mrs. Clay ("Ginny"), and not Margo, who, as the evening wore on, got a little drunk, although on far fewer drinks, and a little pugnacious. With her firm jaw settled and her clear eyes slightly unfocused she tended to make disputes out of discussions. Everyone seemed accustomed to this, however, or in too good a humor to take her seriously.

And yet suddenly I know, without wanting to, I seem to have to know, from my new observation post on this side of the life arch, that this aggressive girl, too, can cry, that a terrible mistrust eats at her, for which even her seven children have not compensated, that she is not at all sure people like her any more than she is sure she likes people.

Zebstrow, you would hardly know me! I hardly know myself. Always before now I looked at men and women briefly and disinterestedly from the outside; or as Branzini said with impatience, "You have the eyes of a sailor watching people come aboard an ocean liner!" which I thought quite picturesque of him. We did not foresee, did we, Zebstrow, that *thinking* would come to bloom like this? Or could it simply be I who comes to bloom, at long last? It frightens me. Am I to discover after all a soul? Is that what responded to the family in the grape arbor?

By common consent we ate out of doors so as not to miss the sunset. Kate had combined subtle-tasting things in an exotic casserole, and I'm not sure what it was we ate, especially in the half-light, but Margo and Simon gravely pronounced approval, and Dr. Clay paid her the greater compliment of asking for more.

The landscape below us turned to a feverish burnt orange. The hills that blocked the level sun's rays threw up clouds of quivering volcanic light, and the sky burst silently into perishing magenta and gold. I remembered Kitty's Indians and the beginning of time, and realized that a sunset, like the moment of ultimate ecstasy between lovers, contains a very plain-spoken statement, as if for an instant we look straight over the rim of life into the cosmic mystery.

I said to Jack, "This was your house, then, before you married Kitty?"

"I never lived in it." His all-seeing eyes lifted from his plate. "It was in my family. Left to me by a relative." And I saw him as the kind of young man relatives willed property to—the hard worker, the promising, the reliable. "I didn't know what to do with it. Nobody lived in it for thirty years. No electricity, no plumbing. Just the way it was a hundred-fifty years ago." He gave me a wry glance. "Then one night I brought Kate up here."

"After you were married?"

"No, before."

"Ah. So this is where you came to get away from Mother."

"I wouldn't put it that way," he told me. "We were sure of privacy, that's all. We had to be alone somewhere."

"Of course." A blanket, perhaps, under the stars; tears, delight. . . . "And Kate fell in love with it?"

He peered through the deepening shadows to her. She was having uphill work making conversation with Dr. Clay, who was occupied with eating his dessert and keeping one ear on his wife's conversation with the Goodfellows at the far end of the terrace, where a boisterous debate was going on. His inattention didn't faze Kitty; she was amused. She looked up at Jack and made a little face, and turned to the doctor again.

"She fell in love with it," Jack reiterated. "She said, 'This house is *yours?*' "

And I felt he must trust me now, because he was confiding in me something he had perhaps never confided in anyone else before. I was Kate's sister, and he wanted Kate to trust me, too.

"Those were her words. Like that. As if she'd found the answer to all her troubles. She said, 'Why, Jack, we could *live* here!' The answer to all our troubles. This house turned the tide. It's a fact." The light, bright eyes shifted to me again. "I don't resent it. I'm glad of it. The fact that this beat-up place of mine made all the difference. She was much calmer after that. It was out of her mother's reach, I guess."

He said to me suddenly, "I don't mean she wouldn't have married me otherwise. This girl is a lot tougher than you might think. And she's come a long way. But a lot of it she had to do alone, in her own mind, I mean, and I'm glad you're back. She needs you."

But a voice cried, "Listen!"

And everyone was still, listening. A sky of pale green lifted before us, fading upward into deep blue, and the woods below, where the pastures ended, were dark, and a whippoorwill was singing there.

"The first of the year!" Kitty breathed. "Oh, this is a *perfect* evening!"

Tentatively, trembling, as if testing the night air, the notes came up to us, and once again I had that sense of explanation, of nearly deciphered statement, and I thought unaccountably, Don't anyone interrupt it, don't anyone answer it—!

And it was then that the first pain began, springing out upon me as if out of the darkness, digging its claws into my guts, so that before I could stop myself I had blurted out a little grunt of protest.

Jack turned to me and I laughed quickly as if I'd let go an impolite noise, and the pain gouged and a headachey flush rose over my forehead, forcing tears of outrage to my eyes, and I was thankful for the half-dark. Somehow I got to my feet.

"Kitty," I said, laughing to cover the gasps in my voice, "forgive me if I eat and run, it's been lovely but you know how I am, I simply have to fold early—"

"Why—of course, darling," she said, rising, and Dr. Clay with her. She was startled and disappointed, but she held my hand between both of hers. "I understand—"

And I had a sensation of surrealism when, having said good night, they all stood motionless like dark pillars, placed meaningfully yet helplessly on the terrace against the green sky, and the bird had stopped singing, and I wanted to tell them, in a madness of pain, Listen! Go on listening, the answer is out there—!

Jack saw me out, his hand protective under my elbow, a baffled questioning in his silence, and Simon Goodfellow innocently followed, saying, "I have to get a closer look at this famous vehicle," and Dr. Clay added reflectively, "Me, too," and while I got seated in the car they prowled around it and would, I'm sure, have been delighted to have me open the hood for a prolonged inspection. Streaming perspiration, I clenched my lip in my teeth to keep back the whimpering within me, and Dr. Clay, pausing to touch my shoulder and remembering his pledge of silence, said quietly, "Hang on. I'll be along soon."

 4 

A week has passed, and I have survived, one might even say won, a battle. Rob Clay wished to hospitalize me, demanded it, but I knew this was only a preliminary skirmish and that I mustn't give way at the first confrontation, and I refused to go.

The earth, the air roared; there was no time lapse. I saw Rob's face by pale daylight and in the next instant it was there in lamplight. I remember grasping his square hand with my right one and the oak-like wrist with my left, and the roaring spun itself out into a high wordless singing like the hum of telephone wires. Bernice's terrified face hovered behind the doctor's shoulder and I asked myself, What is she doing here in Hell?

And at length my adversary wearied and withdrew from the field. I awoke at dawn to an audible and visible peace. Chaste New England summer filtered in the windows, and my bedroom, which had been malevolent, a battleground, was recognizable once more and respectful, the furniture submissive. The fire in my body had gone out.

My mouth opened and a laugh that made no sound

came from it. For a little while I lay perfectly still, waiting, in wonder. Bernice came tiptoeing in from my sitting room and I put out my hand to her. She took it and we were reverently silent for a moment in an Amen. I asked her for breakfast, and with the suggestion of a movement of her shoulders, the nearest thing to a Gallic shrug she dares to make at me, as if she considered it ungracious to begin so simply our old domestic routine again, she went away.

Later that morning Rob came, no longer a disembodied face or an outstretched hand, not even my ally; he delivered me a lecture. I looked at him, remembering how through the lurid smoke of battle he had appeared again and again, to rescue me, albeit disapprovingly, and how I had reached for his hand as if for God's own. Now here he was seated, in his Dacron suit, cross-kneed beside my bed, composed and vexed, aseptic, disappointingly once more the Robert McCracken Clay who was a bit of a pain in the neck, father of seven in his spare time, or should I say fathering seven in his spare time.

I had misbehaved! I had put him and my household through an unnecessary ordeal. Under his reddish brows his blue eyes were severe, admonishing a naughty girl. I had not complied with his standards of treatment and he was put out. And I was embarrassed for him, for I was a victor, cradled in an immense dignity, while he, lecturing on, seemed merely peevish. With bland, idle fatuity, I lay in my bed wondering how I might elevate him, too, to dignity.

And then he brought me bolt upright.

"On your next bout," he told me, concluding his scold, "if you will not agree to hospitalization I will go to Kitty."

"Oh no you won't!" I shouted, rising up.

"Oh yes I shall," he replied, pursing his lips.

"Why you son of a bitch," I commenced tentatively, mustering my wits.

"There is no need," he said, glancing at his wrist watch and uncrossing his knees, "for bad language."

I had to laugh. "Oh really, Rob, come off it!" Bad language indeed; but only Branzini had heard my best gutter words, and they had delighted him. It was amusing; I had grandly aimed at restoring Rob's dignity, whereas he had brought me down, squalling, to an even meaner level. "Oh Rob, you wouldn't, you wouldn't!"

He had risen, and the familiar square hand closed on my wrist, his stern face bent down toward mine, and I actually cowered. "I must, Althea, and I will. I couldn't live with myself as a man and a physician if I let you go through this again. In this week you may have wasted many precious days of your life. Don't you see, my dear girl: I can prolong your life if you will let me."

I fell back, sickened, and turned away. "Don't you see, Robert McCracken Clay," I moaned, "I do not want my life prolonged."

He hesitated, breathing thoughtfully and medicinally over me. Then he said, "What you want to do with your life now is not really in your hands any more. It's useless to be emotional about it."

The words chilled me to the bone. I turned and sat up again slowly, peering into his rational eyes, and he, relenting, perched for a moment on the bed beside me; after all, we had been through battle together, and this was not to be discounted. "Stay with me," I pleaded. He still held my wrist in his sensible grasp. "I'm not nearly as unafraid as I seem to be. No matter what I say or do, stand by me!"

He gave me an amused, paternal smile. (And I, a few minutes ago, had been so much older than he, a thousand years older!) He stated, "You are still trying to play on my sympathies, and I still mean what I said."

"Oh damn you!" I wrenched my wrist away, and then I clutched his hand in both of mine before he could remove himself. "Listen, darling." I shut my eyes, trying to think, leaning my cheek against his hand. "I've got a lot to make up with Kitty. We never knew each other very well. I can't do it if she knows about this damned leukemia. That would color everything. One can forgive a dying person anything, a dying person can forgive anything. Self-revelation becomes superficial. I would never reach her through all that morbidity. This is important! It's all I have to do. And what's more important, possibly, is that she could never reach me. Yes, you see: I have to be found, and perhaps she needs to reveal herself, too."

I opened my eyes and he was still smiling. He did not withdraw his hand. He said, "Don't underestimate your sister."

"Oh God," I sighed, and released him, "you are a fundamentalist, aren't you? Do I have to get to first base with you, too?" But he had made a disturbing point: did I underestimate Kitty?

"No," he answered cheerfully, "you don't. Now, rest in bed today, and don't try to go out or do anything active for several days, and if there's any recurrence of pain I trust you to let me know at once. Take your medication." He reached for his medicine bag. "Turn over, I'm going to give you an injection." And thus he robbed me of my last ounce of dignity.

I am lying on the chaise in my sitting room. The latticed shutters are closed against the sun and the greenish submarine light is soothing; stripes of light and shadow ride across my feet.

The room is just as it was when I was a girl. Mother wanted to do it over for me but I wouldn't let her. There is even a bowl of roses in the center of the white wicker table in the center of the room, and I can almost see Mother arranging them, her pale oval face devout as it always was when she tended flowers, her long lashes downcast, her fingers moving prayerfully among the leaves.

She would come into my room and do this, into anyone's room, and with her closed face she seemed to say, Pay no attention to me, I am invisible, I am at my devotions. And when at last she stepped back, making a final head-tilting inspection, and looked up, a surprised smile would light up her face: I hadn't realized you were here! She would put *you* in the position of intruding on *her*.

I had an unpleasant habit of looking back at her without speaking. It was my only defense, I suppose. In my idle moments, which were many even then, I read, and she found it exasperating that I could withdraw so completely into books. She had long ago given up trying to engage me in conversation, and she resorted to finding excuses to indulge in monologues that she pretended were conversations. Oh God, it was pitiful, I suppose, and hideous, like all sly, obscure family games, and yet some cruelty in me, or honesty, will not shirk from recalling it now. It's as if I can only uncover myself as I am by remembering her as she was.

I see her standing back from her flowers and smiling, and when I as usual say nothing her gaze wanders, she puts a finger to her chin, she casts her eyes about the room, looks at the matching white wicker furniture, the faded cretonne cushions on the window seats on each side of the little moss-green fireplace, and she begins, "Really, darling, we ought to do this room over. It really has got awfully shabby."

I wait in silence. *We* do the room over? Another pretense; *she* would do the room over, around my supine body, just as she had the dressmaker make me those silk dresses, or arranged a party for me, or ordered a special health-building diet for me—another excuse, as well, for endless monologues. And why, I wondered, was she anxious to do over my sitting room when she was so vengefully indifferent to the rest of the house, grimly preserving its ugliness?

"Green!" she exclaims. "Aren't you tired of green, darling? These green walls! It's a stain, I believe, not a paint; it was meant to look rustic, but it's rather depressing, don't you think, it absorbs the light so." Her deep brown eyes move to claim me again, she smiles encouragingly for her own sake. "Can you see it in pale blue? I see it in pale blue, since you get the sun in the afternoon. It would be cool, yet not so dark. We could have the furniture painted to match—or no, why not get rid of these clumsy wicker things altogether? A pale blue rug, and something more delicate in furniture, French provincial perhaps, with a pretty chintz, and of *course* new curtains—"

I speak. I open my mouth and she comes to an abrupt halt. Dully yet firmly I say, "I like it this way."

She is flabbergasted. I have expressed myself! She is almost intimidated; she makes a huge mental readjustment. Does she really care for my taking a stand? "You actually like it this way?"

I have spoken; I speak no more. I stare at her. Oh yes, I was impossible too; a pair of us.

"Fancy that!" She is rather at sea, unable to decide whether she is flattered or thwarted. "The way Mama and Papa had it done for me?" She is smiling again. I can't imagine why she must triumph in this way. I don't try. I suffer her to do so. To take part in conversation with her is to engage in a contest, guileful and entangling. "You knew that, didn't you, darling? This room is *exactly* as Mama and Papa had it done for me. You haven't forgotten this was my own childhood sitting room?"

I haven't forgotten and I haven't remembered. What difference does it make? It's a room, that's all, and I spend a lot of time in it. I can't keep her out of it, but I can prevent her turning it upside down in a pretense of doing me a favor.

She is off again. Her hands reach out to hover over her flowers as if warming them at a fire. "They were like that, Mama and Papa. Nothing was too good for me. They loved doing sweet things for me, to make me feel loved, cherished, their only child. Oh, they spoiled me—!"

Am I supposed to blame myself for not cherishing and spoiling her? She's mad, I think, in the manner of my nineteenth-century novelists; the woman is mad.

And for some reason I don't believe it, either, that her Mama and Papa spoiled her. I think of them as well-meaning but obtuse, and somewhat unfeeling, and their only child as very lonely.

"Yes, how odd of you," she says, renewing the attack. "You never were a sentimental person in any way; in fact I am surprised when you notice *anything*. Now *Katherine*—" and at once her voice changes, her throat fills as if with bile, tightens just beneath the curve of her jaw, "*Katherine* is the one who hangs onto things, invests everything with so much emotion." Her voice, speaking of Katherine, drops lower and lower until she sounds almost calm, much less girlish and arch, a voice unconsciously stabilized by its burden of bitterness.

"Her dreadful animals, for instance—do you remember how she nursed her pets into decrepit old age? That dog, do you remember him, the fat shiny one that smelled so? She didn't say a word when I put him to sleep, and that was when she stopped collecting pets, although I didn't tell her she must, but of course I *knew* she was heartbroken, just the way she looked at me without saying a word when I told her, turned around and walked away without saying a word. . . ."

My God, is she going to cry about it, here and now? Her voice has dropped to a broken whisper. Am I supposed to feel bad because she never poisoned any of *my* pets? Because I never had any pets, at all, as Katherine did? Warningly I draw up my knees and resettle my book.

She brightens, she laughs her subhysterical laugh, she sucks in a little saliva that has gathered at the corners of her lips, she lifts her palms, open-fingered, from the flowers, as if to say, I concede to you, I always concede to you! "I *am* pleased. I really am pleased that you want to keep my shabby little room just as it is, just as Mama and Papa did it for me!" She isn't pleased, that's obvious, and yet she ends on a note, again, of triumph.

But still she doesn't leave. Her eyes wander, drop, and for an instant a genuine chill seems to touch her. She is alone, a lovely faded woman long ago deserted by her husband. Mama and Papa are long dead, much water has gone over the dam, she has no one but a daughter she did not want who presents her with the thankless task of trying to tolerate her, and another she tries to idolize who will not take part with her in the simplest chat. . . .

Once more she recovers herself. "I'll leave you to your book. Mrs. Mainwaring is coming to tea with her niece, such a plain girl, poor thing. Do be an angel and come down for a moment. Katherine will be there of course." And automatically she adds the phrase that by now makes the hair rise on the back of my neck: "She is my dutiful daughter and you are my beautiful one!" And she turns and glides away, leaving behind her the scent of lily of the valley, and for a few moments the printed words writhe before my eyes.

Did I dream this, or make it up? How can I possibly remember every word, every inflection, as if it had just happened? What is so important about it? And yet this is how she still exists for me. Gently and sweetly she still intrudes, usurping my attention, my patience, my very liver, my sick blood!

Perhaps I begin to realize these oppressive monologues were not really so trivial, that something was going on in her, behind them, all the while. She was demanding something of me I couldn't give, she was telling me something she dared not put in words, and her sweet, gay, brave ramblings were punishing. "You must love me!" she seemed to insist.

Or no; no. More likely this: "I must love you. I insist on loving you. I must not hate you!"

Once, I suddenly remember now, she opened my sitting room door to leave and found Katherine outside it in the hall and struck her so hard on the neck that Katherine reeled, thumping, against the opposite wall. Katherine never listened at doors. Probably she was just about to knock, and Mother must have known this.

I hear Zebstrow ask, "Well, what do you think?"

I think, my friend, that Mother's rage was not for Katherine. I think it had accumulated in this room and merely found an object.

There was more to that scene outside my door. When Katherine had regained her footing she turned, all at once gracefully, white-faced, to Mother. She was in her early teens, the bones of her cheeks and nose just beginning to draw her face out of amorphous softness. And the words she uttered quietly came out like this: "Don't. You. Ever. Touch. Me. Again."

She went into her room, opposite mine, and softly shut the door. And although Mother continued to drive her with words, she never did touch her again, in blow or caress.

It's only natural, I suppose, that details should come back to me here at Northwater that I couldn't remember for Zebstrow. "We skip over your mother so glibly," he complained, "too glibly. Yes, she bored you, she bores you now, she even bores me. We dwell on your father instead. We have examined him inside and out; I see him quite clearly wearing spats on Sunday on Fifth Avenue. You cater too willingly to the theories of my profession: mothers of sons, fathers of daughters—

the great influences. But I, Zebstrow, have a theory of my own: the mothers of daughters cast the darkest shadow."

One night during the past week, perhaps in a lull of the battle with pain, when I was heavily drugged and susceptible, I thought I heard a whispering, low and insistent. It seemed to come from outside my window. I listened but I couldn't make out the words. It went on and on.

I moaned for Bernice; I lurched up, drenched with sweat, weak with drugs, and screamed for her. She came running in, hair awry, making for the capsules by my bedside. "No," I screamed. "The window, the window! Who is there?"

"My God," she screamed back at me, in French, "no one is there, who would be there? The wind is blowing and it is raining!"

"Shut the window!" I ordered her. "Lock it! Draw the shade, draw the curtains!" I buried my head in the pillows, and she did as she was told, and then came to give me my medicine. I quieted at last and told her she could go.

"I will stay until you sleep," she said. Stony-faced, she sponged my neck and arms. Whatever her sexual tendencies, which I have long suspected, they are so thoroughly repressed that one might almost call her emasculated. "It was the rain," she told me soothingly. "It was the rain running down through the drain pipe. Do you hear it any more?"

"No," I told her, sighing, growing drowsy. "She's

gone now."

Bernice's voice came softly. "She?"

"Yes, she. My mother. She was trying to tell me something. Oh God, don't open the window again. Good night, Bernice. . . ."

I had just finished writing these words, this afternoon, when there was a light tap on my sitting room door and Kitty walked in.

I stared at her open-mouthed. "Kitty! You walked in, you came into the house!"

She was pale, a little short of breath, her eyes huge, and she leaned against the door she had shut behind her and gave a quick sigh of relief. She focused on me through the greenish semidarkness. "You *are* all right, Althea?"

So it was for me that she had entered Northwater again, made the journey down the hall and up the stairs, alone. "Of course I'm all right." But I was thankful for the half-light.

"I called two or three times. Bernice told me you were resting and didn't want to be disturbed. I don't mean to be a nuisance, Althea, but I was worried."

"You mustn't worry, Kitty. I've told you, I have to rest a lot, and I'm not terribly sociable, you know that. I have these spells and then I snap out of them. Do sit down. I'm glad you've come. I'm terribly impressed. You came right in!"

"Bernice offered to announce me," she said evasively,

moving to a wicker chair, "but I told her I could find my way." She looked young and comely, her feet in sandals, the soft folds of her blue dress falling about her knees as she sat facing me. Fresh with health, she was a visitor to my dim morbid sitting room from an antithetical world, and I again had a sense of good news, of something sane and solid and heart-healing having been bestowed on me, and I was thankful for her, as if she were a blessing I'd forgotten I possessed—my sister, real, alive, of the present time.

But I wouldn't let her off so easily. There must be no more evasions between us than we could help. "You didn't meet Mother's ghost?"

She winced a little and answered, "No," as if I'd asked a literal question. Then she made a humorous grimace. "Although I expected to at every turn."

"I know," I told her. "I still do, too. And how about guilt feelings?"

She shrank, she wished not to talk about it; her eyes roamed. "I just felt—overpowered. It *is* an overpowering house, isn't it? All those moose heads staring down at one through the gloom, and the pipes towering at the end of the hall. It takes one's breath away; there wasn't *room* to feel anything about myself. It's so very still, Althea. It's like stealing into a natural history museum after closing hours."

I laughed. (Was she still being evasive?) "Well, good for you, Kitty. You're over that hump."

"Yes." But her eyes roamed about the room as if fearful of discovering something she didn't wish to remember, and sure enough, they fastened with a start on Mother's little pink-enameled clock ticking quietly on the mantel.

I said, "How is Jack?"

That restored her. Her face changed in a flash. "Jack is fine!" She smiled at me, her eyes softening, as if to say, Yes, Jack, thank God!

"I haven't talked to you since your supper party. I enjoyed it, Kitty, and you are a very skillful and charming hostess."

"Why, thank you, Althea. Did you like the Goodfellows? They thought you were wonderful, although I think they're a little in awe of you. Margo sounded me out as to whether you might come to lunch some Sunday; she's going to ask you. You must see their house. It was a deserted mill hanging over a stream, but the way they've done it over inside isn't at all what you'd expect."

I told her I certainly wouldn't expect anything conventional of the Goodfellows.

In awe of me? It's not the first time I've heard this. Is it because I've always been inclined to be somewhat impassive, not given to small talk, not needing to assert myself? Branzini, the most confident of men, told me he was in awe, when he first met me.

I was under the wing of Mrs. Maxim then, Mother's old school friend who lived in Rome on the *piano nobile* of an ancient palazzo. She was a warty old toad, decorated with beads and pins and rings, but beloved, for under her hard drive and her acid tongue there beat a very sentimental old heart, which everyone knew would give out suddenly one day. And it did, but not before she had introduced me to everyone she thought worth knowing. I often felt we were like patroness and protégée in a Henry James novel, lacking only carriages and parasols in our comings and goings, our rigorously observed amenities, our private gossip, our calculated moves.

For she had decided I was to burst upon the Roman scene, after the proper training, as a kind of celebrity, who comes from nowhere, has accomplished nothing, yet rivets attention through her own look of self-justification. It was uphill work but she pulled it off, capitalizing on my passivity, my pallor, even the faintly dislocated look of tragedy. For without realizing it I was still in something of a state of shock from what had happened at Northwater. She insisted on my learning languages, she moved me about Europe so that there wasn't a capital or an in-vogue village I hadn't inhabited, she drummed elegance—her favorite word—into me. And at the end of a year she pronounced me presentable. "You were never exactly a sow's ear, my dear, but we can now safely say you are a silk purse."

And having launched me, her romantic nature couldn't resist matchmaking, and it was to one of her soirées that she lured Branzini.

"There he is," she leaned sideways to mutter in my ear, "against the wall, listening to Señora Higgins. Already he has his eye on you. No, don't turn your head, he has been pursued enough, he is gorged with offerings. Two years a widower, and all those factories in Turin! Thank God you wore white tonight; on you it is so ethereal. Yes, he *is* definitely taking you in. Oh, those smoldering eyes! Of course you realize I get a vicarious thrill out of this. Too proud to be introduced, is he? Then let him wait!" And she sat back complacently, fanning air into her gasping lungs, her lids drooping over her bulging eyes.

"I was in awe of you. I, Branzini, was in awe." Thus he informed me afterward. "I had had my fill," he said in all seriousness, "of hot-blooded beauties. My wife," he added, "among them. A Sicilian, naturally." He frowned into the distance as if recalling pain. "And there you were, cool and fair as a lily, yet looking as if nothing could surprise you, and I knew I had to discover for myself the appetites, if there were any, beneath that cool delicacy." Even had I not been an heiress, he told me, he would have had to own me. "I knew in that moment that I must be able to look across a roomful of people and tell myself, 'She is mine, she belongs to me, whether she sleeps in the afternoons with someone else or not, I have only to lift an eyebrow and she goes home with me.' "

The really original thing—and this Branzini found it impossible to believe—was that I never did sleep in the afternoons, while I was his wife, with someone else.

Kitty's hands were tensed again on the arms of the wicker chair. We had been silent for some moments. An insect, caught between shutter and screen, buzzed fitfully. "We have so much to say to each other, Kitty. We've never really got started."

"I'm afraid I put you off the afternoon of my party."

"I've put you off, too."

"It wasn't as if there were a great hurry. I've waited a long time, all my life, in fact. But you've changed, Althea, or maybe it's just that we're both older; I can feel so much closer to you. I felt I could ask you about Daddy."

"Kitty, I warn you, my feelings about him are awfully mixed—were awfully mixed. Remember, too, I was only seven when he left and I never saw him again. Dr. Zebstrow in Zurich put it this way: 'You were in love with him and he rejected you.' Ho, ho! Doesn't that sound academic? But, I mean, it may not do you much good, to hear about him from me. Sarah Hodge worked here in Daddy's day. She knew him, too. You should ask her about him."

"I did. She didn't give much." Kitty's dark brows knitted over her probing eyes. "Maybe she has mixed feelings about him, too."

"Maybe we're afraid if we start talking about him we'll make you despise him."

"Oh dear." Kitty shrank back in her chair, her knuckles whitening.

"Oh yes. He was a bit of a scoundrel. Surely you must have guessed that. He could be quite unrepentantly cruel. But he was adorable, too," I added, my voice quickening, "he was truly lovable—charming, winning!" I could sing him an ode of love or I could prick the bubble of my own myth of him, or both at the same time, and no one could make me pause to consider, as Zebstrow had, and for once I could make him real again.

An irresponsible excitement possessed me. Zebstrow was a wise receptacle but neuter, after all, a stranger at the beginning and at the end, and his Russo-Germanic gravity made me weigh my words with unusual care. I was in Northwater now, where every door and turn of a corridor opened on some all-but-forgotten memory, and I had no one to answer to, and my listener was my own sister, whose father was mine, and she would have to take him as he came from me.

"He was aware, Kitty; that was the interesting thing about him, he was aware of what was going on around him, of how people felt. He would know how *you* felt, what you were like inside, on first meeting. He would have understood Jack, and liked him from the start. It wasn't so much sensitivity as a kind of clever intuition, a power of divination, perhaps merely a way of measuring himself and where he stood with others."

I could hear myself spilling out words with abandon, and I was amazed but helpless, as if some floodgate had been lifted, or I'd been administered a truth drug.

"You see, he could use this awareness delightfully, to delight others, and he could use it cruelly. Poor Mother, she was the *least* aware person I've ever known, even less than I was, and he made life miserable for her, a lot of the time without trying. But then, if he hadn't been so much more clever, she would have made life miserable for him. She made life miserable for everyone else *but* Daddy."

Kitty said, very softly, "Did she?"

I had almost forgotten Kitty, except as a mute, shadowy listener. "Well, didn't she?"

"She made life miserable for you, too, Althea?"

"She didn't make it a thing of beauty, love. Did you think she had? How could she?"

"But you were—" Kitty hesitated.

"Her favorite? Well, I'm beginning to wonder. Let's not get sidetracked. If we get onto the subject of Mother we'll never get off it. We'd better stick to Daddy."

"Tell me—tell me what he looked like. What he looked like to you."

I studied her through the striped, submarine light. "He looked like you. You must know that, too. He was small of build, or slight, not quite as tall as Mother when she had heels on, and he was dark and quick, light on his feet. He dressed fastidiously, maybe a trifle vulgarly, more like a musical comedy star than a New York club member. He was good at almost anything—tennis, hunting, polo—and he was forever taking up something new, fencing or gliding or whatever, and he was smart at cards, and he could play the piano quite amusingly by ear. He *had* to be good at everything; maybe he had a tiny little inferiority complex, or maybe he just knew he *could* be good at it."

I laughed. "Am I making him sound dreadful? Ah, but you can't imagine his charm, the dark laughing eyes, the way he immediately got through a person's shell—

a stiff old lady, or a little boy in the park. . . ." I mused a moment. "But you know, for all that there was this touch of vulgarity about him, he had an odd sort of—aristocraticness, is there such a word?—a tension, an intensity, a rightness of self-determination. How can I describe it? It was perverse. It certainly was anything but moral, or honorable, but it was a kind of integrity. He couldn't be compromised, or compromise himself. There was more nobility in him, in a sense, than there was in Mother, for all her ladylike upbringing."

Kitty was watching me with a new expression. I noticed it even through the dim light and my own excitement: not as if she saw Daddy for the first time but as if she were seeing me in a new way, a double image, perhaps—her father's daughter superimposed on her father. Without my intending it, the recreation of Kitty's unknown father was becoming a recreation of her unknown sister.

She said, "Tell me how he was with you."

"He adored me, and I adored him!" I held my breath for an instant. "If he spoiled me it wasn't with ulterior motives, like Mother!" I made an impatient sigh. "No, that's not true." I shook my head, smiling. "I have a picture of us walking up Fifth Avenue, I in a white rabbit's-fur coat, with a white fur hat and a white fur muff, white gloves and white leggings and white *rubbers,* can you believe it, and my hair hanging down my back, and Daddy very dashing in a Homburg and an overcoat with a sable collar—my God, we must have looked like old-time movie stars. People smiled at us and we smiled back, like royalty, smug as you please, hand in hand. And he would take me to the Plaza for lunch, or to the old Sherry's to show me off to his girl friends, and quite often to a matinee, even to the opera, and he had everyone bowing and scraping and beaming at us. Oh, it was quite a game, the prince and his fairy princess!"

"Girl friends, Althea?"

"Kitty, don't interrupt! If you make me lose my train of thought I'll never be able to—yes, girl friends, girl friends! New ones, old ones. Like his cars, a quick turnover, paid for with Mother's money." I stopped, caught my breath, tried to still my anger. "It isn't true, he did have ulterior motives. It was a way of saying, Who needs you? to the impatient girls who complicated his life, the contemptuous wife who yearned to subdue him, the substantial people who must have snubbed him. How they glared at me, with their mascaraed eyes, the girls waiting at Sherry's! And he grinned at them, saying, 'I brought my little sweetheart, my best girl, I knew you'd love her, isn't she adorable?' and I grinned, too—"

I stopped, listening to the echoing harshness of my voice. A throbbing heat burned over my eyelids and temples.

"And then he would go away," I resumed at last, dully. "He would just be—gone. He must have made preparations but he didn't give me any warning or say good-by. I would just wake up and find he had taken off somewhere—to Africa or Alaska or Paris or Peking, and weeks would go by, and I would receive a few funny, uncontrite post cards, and Mother would go into her act—beautiful young Mother putting up a brave front. . . . But I, I was sick at heart, betrayed. After all that indulgence and closeness, as though nothing on earth could part us, to be suddenly *left*, without a good-by! And then I got used to it. I must have suspected he wouldn't come home at all some day. That was when I began to clam up. I just couldn't speak to anyone much, and it got to be permanent. I felt like a zero, I lived in a zero."

Kitty didn't move, or make a sound, and I couldn't tell what she was thinking, or care.

"So that by the time he died in London, of heart disease, of all things, I wasn't grief-stricken. I was long numb. Mother was more shaken than I was. It isn't hard to imagine that his death deprived her of something—her martyrdom, for one thing; but perhaps she hoped he would come back to her, hoped through some magic to love him—I don't know. But *I* thought, He's got what he deserves."

"Oh, Althea—!" Kitty protested in a whisper.

"Yes, it was vengeful, childish, but I meant it. I was glad he was dead! I didn't have to hope any more. I could close up my feelings for him for good."

"Could you, Althea? Could you, really?"

"Oh, don't—!" Thin watery tears, like drops distilled from vapor, suddenly sprang out, prickling, in the back of my eyes and throat. Why must she keep breaking in? I sighed angrily, cleared my throat, reached trembling for a cigarette, and Kitty waited in silence, only her eyebrows expressing commiseration. "Well, obviously not,"

I conceded, smiling, once more in control of myself, protected within the layers of time. "But I did as good a job as I was able. A very good job of it. Now and then he appeared in a dream, but I didn't think of him willingly, and seldom consciously, for years."

We were silent again. I sensed that Kitty was reserving judgment. The little room was stuffy. My lids and temples were damp with perspiration now. I thought longingly of rest.

Kitty stirred. "Do you want to stop?"

"What more do you want to know?"

"Did he ever love Mother at all?"

"I think so. I think he might very well have been head over heels in love with her at first; she was a beautiful woman, tall, refined, rich. And I think he might have stayed in love with her if she'd been capable of loving. Her mama and papa must have siphoned off that capacity in her. She evidently had a very airless, humorless Victorian upbringing. It made her somewhat dense, and he, being clever and intuitive, teased her unmercifully."

"Teased her?"

"Tormented her."

I cleared my dry throat. "I'll give you an example that pretty well sums it up. Something that happened here at Northwater."

My head was bowed over my folded arms. I had to force the words, now, and they came slowly. "Daddy had arrived for the weekend. The hydroplane he chartered from New York had deposited him on the dock.

He went upstairs to change, and we waited for him on the veranda, Mother and I. She was wearing one of her chiffon tea gowns, all pale pointed draperies, and she wore a fixed welcoming smile, a variation of her long-suffering smile, and we sat there in silence. When she wrapped herself in this role it was no use saying anything to her. She couldn't hear, or wouldn't answer; the stillness surrounding her was almost holy. Beads of sweat gathered on Daddy's silver cocktail shaker and Mother's pitcher of iced tea; she wouldn't drink with him, of course. That would have been a form of surrender.

"And he came running lightly down at last and joined us, freshly showered, tanned and handsome in summer flannels, and as usual he had a present for me and one for Mother. And I knew at once he was up to mischief because he was wearing his little smile, a smile mostly in the eyes, a deep glowing, and I saw that Mother's present was done up in white satin ribbons with a little sprig of artificial lily of the valley, and I realized it was wrapped like a wedding gift. I thought for a moment she was going to refuse to take it from his hands, but perhaps she hoped it really was a lover's gift, a peace offering, and she laughed nervously and took it, and opened it, and there was a lot of tissue paper, and finally she got to the present. It was the revolver, Kitty. The little pearl-handled revolver."

Kitty, stiffening, uttered a gasp that just lacked the tonal quality of a scream, and her hands flew to her mouth.

"Yes, the revolver. She had evidently asked him for

one, probably because she was alone so much in this great house. But when she unwrapped it from all the tissue paper she flushed and thrust it away from her, box and all, and leaped up, facing him. And he lounged gracefully with his hands in his pockets and said, 'Isn't it what you wanted, dearest?' His eyes laughed into hers, and I, knowing he had perpetrated some kind of joke, laughed too. I didn't understand it then, of course, but I laughed. 'To keep in your bed?' he said. 'To keep off the invaders of the night?' Her face blanched as white as the bridal ribbons and tissue. Even Mother couldn't mistake the symbolism of it. She put up her hands, the way you do when you want to say, It's finished, it's done, and turned and went inside. Was that before or after your conception, I wonder? It's remarkable she didn't use the revolver then, the day he gave it to her."

I half-collapsed forward, my fists on my knees. "Oh, Kitty, forgive me. I've said too much. I knew it wasn't a good idea. My own feelings are too much involved. Forgive me if I've upset you."

She was sitting with her shoulders hunched as I had seen her do before, her hands clasped in her lap. And I realized she wasn't really upset at all, but lost in thought. This had happened when she didn't exist, she was not involved. She said at last in her low voice: "I pity them."

Wise Kitty. Kitty, the tender-hearted. I studied her. How could I have imagined her capable of violence?

The room was still for a long time. And then Bernice, who is *not* above listening at doors, knocked at just the right moment and came in with a tray of refreshments.

I wonder. I wonder what it was, even though in fantasy, through fever and rain, that Mother was trying to tell me?

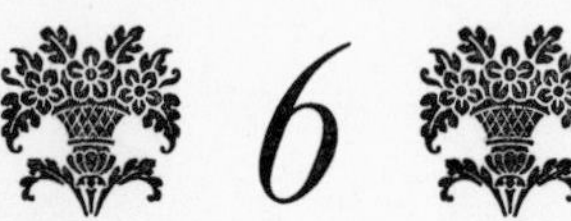

My first day out of the house since Kitty's party. Early morning. June. The sun up, the lawns covered with dew, birds singing. Clarence Hodge was working quietly on his hands and knees in Mother's rose garden as I passed on my way to the dock.

"Morning, Clarence."

He lifted his seamed, leathery face. "Monnin', Althea." Among the old-timers it's a courtesy and a mark of some affection to address a person by his first name. Clarence probably knew all about me, in my flagrant days, in the way that the natives always were able to size up the summer people, and yet I think he liked me as some men cannot help a fondness for a young girl, however iniquitous. A sinewy, proud-eyed man, he must once have been quite a Lothario himself. "Fine day," he said.

"Yes, a fine day. How are you, Clarence?"

"Slicker'n a cat's wrist." The old colloquialisms fell easily from his lips like echoes of history. "Seems natural, you comin' down from the house for your monnin' dip."

"I keep coming back, don't I?"

"Ayah. Always knew *some*body would come back." His great earth-wedded hands moved again, plucking weeds. "Always knew it wa'n't the end of things."

He had finished talking to me and I moved on. A little breeze pressed over the lake, just enough to ruffle the water and pick up its fragrance.

There was always to be, did he mean, a reckoning?

I strolled back to the house, rubbing my hair with a towel. It loomed before me, turrets, roofs, lowering eaves, but its windows were opened wide to the sun, for Sarah Hodge was cleaning; my agony-steeped pillows were hung over the sill to purify, a dimity curtain in Mother's dressing-room tower fluttered outside its casement as if gaily signaling me—Come in, come back, she's gone! Mixed accents gossiped over the clatter of breakfast dishes, kitchen sounds that wouldn't carry to the front of the house but for the stillness and the open windows. "Ah *non*," Bernice's brittle voice asserted indisputably, "never with linen or lingerie!" Other voices joined in, chanting a kind of chorale to detergents, with a continuo of rattling silver, and then there was sudden inexplicable laughter, followed by sudden inexplicable silence.

Yes, the house was all benevolence, spread open there in the sun. Whatever words and dark deeds had been perpetrated within, their lingering vibrations were dispersed in floods of sunlit air. I could hear the telephone ringing and Sarah Hodge answering it in her desperate telephone voice, but I couldn't make out the words. Ping . . . ping . . . the wind chimes, turning slowly, sang their little song over the veranda.

All was cheerful, industrious, expurgative.

"Now *thy*-ah," announced Sarah as I came up the stairs. It was her Yankee way of saying, Now *there*, a phrase she uses for greeting, for approval, for disapproval, for philosophizing. She stood stolidly above me with her fist grasping her mop at arm's length like a Wagnerian soprano on a Valhallan eminence. "And I just got through tellin' him you was down t' the *dock*." (*Dawk*, she pronounced it.) "Jack Gilman, 'twas, at the gara*dge*. Says your station wagon's ready and waitin', says he's been tryin' to get hold of you. I told him I didn't know nothin' '*bout* it. Said you'd call him *ba*-ack." When a sentence doesn't scan she adds an extra syllable. "Now thy-ah, you're lookin' ever so much better. Look al-most like your old self. *Skin* shines. Used t' say t' Clarence, back-along, you was fifteen-sixteen, her skin *shi*-ines."

Without thinking, without a word, I rested my hand on her heavy shoulder, with its starched apron strap, and my face against her cheek, soft as floured dough. She represented something durable from the past, the sanity of durability, something patient and forgiving. We drew apart and stared at each other, startled: had I never before demonstrated affection for her? "Now thy-ah," she said, gently. I smiled and moved on down the hall.

But instead of turning in at my own door I passed it, took the turn of the corridor, and went on to Mother's room. I had looked into it since my arrival. I made myself look into almost every nook and cranny of the house, but I hadn't actually stepped into Mother's room, and I was quite aware, now, that I was taking advantage of the sunlight and the open windows and the temporary banishment of horror.

Sarah and her helpers had been thorough. The spread and the white canopy over the bed were freshly laundered. Mahogany gleamed; even the brass drawer-pulls shone. In the middle of the big quiet room I stood still for a moment, as though listening. "Mmm-aaah!" someone sang vagrantly below, in a melodious sigh. Very softly, as if I were invisible, I crossed the Turkish carpet to the tower and the dressing room.

A semicircular dressing table fits beneath the latticed windows, and the glass top frames a covering of white lace. The sunlight glinted in the deeply carved silver toilet set—short- and long-handled mirrors, brushes, powder and pin boxes, nail scissors, buffer, shoe horn, button hook. The silver-filigreed vases, which used always to hold white roses, still stood on each side of the mirror stand. Only the little pink-enameled clock, its pink leather case opening like cathedral doors, was missing. It was the one possession of Mother's that I had taken away with me. Daddy had bought it for her at Cartier's in Paris on their honeymoon.

I stood smiling, my finger to my lips. This is where they found her.

She was bent over the dressing table, her head abjectly bowed on it, the little clock ticking on imperiously, the small pearl-handled revolver still warm. Time stopped in this room and instantly began again.

Perhaps that is why, gratefully, I took the little clock. I moved now to unhook the dimity curtain, which had caught on the open window, and I stood for a moment looking down on lawns and gardens.

"You are gone," I said softly. "You are gone, you are gone!"

It was a lovely morning.

Then suddenly there was a preliminary sputter, an annunciatory roar, and Clarence Hodge commenced his grand processional with the power mower.

I telephoned Jack, and by the time I was dressed and had come downstairs he was waiting in the drive with the old station wagon.

"Sorry you were under the weather," he said. The morning sun was behind him and his face and body were in silhouette. "You *look* good."

"Thank you, Jack. You didn't have to wait out here. Would you like some coffee?"

"No thanks. I'll be getting back." But he was reluctant to leave the station wagon without some recognition from me. "She looks pretty nice, doesn't she?"

"Handsome!" I exclaimed appropriately. "Practically brand new."

"Well, as Carlton says, she *is* practically brand new." He caressed the car's shining flanks. "See, for one thing, the salt has never got to her, the salt they put down on the roads here in winter."

"I'll will her to you, Jack," I said lightly.

"All right," he answered in kind, "and meanwhile take good care of her."

It was quiet again, for Clarence had stopped mowing, and the scent of freshly cut grass rose under the warming sun. I was aware of the idle charm of conversing out of doors on a summer morning with a friend, our voices lowered as if the space we occupied gave us privacy, like a room, and I thought Jack must have come under this spell too, for he seemed in no hurry to leave. He said, patting the fender again, "This is a little bit like the first time I brought her out."

"When you fell in love with Kate." Automatically I call my sister Kate when I'm with Jack.

"I guess I already was in love with her. Or put it this way: I was just waiting for the chance to fall in love with her." Then he drove his fist gently against the palm of his other hand in a punctuating way, closing the subject. "Your roses are coming into bloom. Ours aren't out yet. It's cooler up there."

"Would you like to take some for Kate?"

"Why yes, I would. I can keep them in water at the office. I don't want to hold you up though."

"You're not holding me up. I'll get some clippers."

"I've got a knife. That'll do just as well."

We moved down over the lawn and in under the trellis gate to the rose garden. It seemed warmer in this enclosure with the light blinding, and bees hummed in unison with the sun's vibrations. "Nice," said Jack, his eyes half-shut and his hands in his pockets, as much at home in a garden as a garage. He took out a fat knife, selected a blade, and set to work cutting roses, handling both knife and stems expertly.

I strolled from bush to bush behind him. "And how do you think Kate is now?"

He straightened, gazed across the beds. He understood the question and didn't quibble over it. "You could say she's better. Not so upset, I mean. Maybe she *is* over the worst of it. But she's different."

"Still haunted?"

He gave me his little smile; the word was too fanciful for him. "She's quieter. I think, for the first time, she's got something on her mind she can't talk to me about."

"She's still feeling guilty?"

"Guilty?" His hand holding the roses dropped to his side and color started into his cheek bones. "What the hell has she got to feel guilty about?" It was a protest rather than a question. He said, "You know, I cornered her mother here, right here in this rose garden. I tracked her down and cornered her."

"Good lord." I couldn't help smiling. "To ask for Kate's hand in marriage?"

"Not exactly. I asked her, I wanted to ask her, to give Kate a break, with or without me. Oh, I disremember, I was just mad, I guess. Kate was in such a terrible state, not eating, not sleeping, nobody to take her side, her mother threatening suicide—" He lifted the roses again, put them to his nose, and inhaled their fragrance deeply. "Well, it didn't do any good of course, my talking to Mrs. North. She wouldn't even look at me."

I studied him, his out-thrust ears with the sun shining through them, his long lashes, longer than Kate's or mine, his wiry arms below the rolled-up sleeves. He had an odor, fine and stringent, like pine needles, or laundry soap, or cologne. Mother didn't need to look at him to know he was thoroughly masculine, however vulgar.

"That's what made me so mad, finally," Jack said, the anger gone from his voice. "She was cutting roses, she had a big straw hat on, and she kept her eyes lowered the whole time I was talking to her, trying to make her see reason. I came here meaning to ease the situation, but after ten minutes of following her around and not being looked at I finally lost my temper in spite of myself, and I got right in front of her so she couldn't move without sidestepping, and I said," Jack laughed softly now, "I said, 'Mrs. North, don't *be* like this!' That's all I could think of to say!" He shook his head. "I was a lot younger then and a lot cockier, though a lot less sure of myself."

"And what did she answer?"

"She didn't. She just stood there, like a queen, waiting for me to get out of her way. And I said, 'This isn't helping Katherine any!' She shut her eyes. She said, '*Help . . . Katherine?*' Like that; like, Now I've heard everything." His clear eyes stared at me pleadingly, with sorrow and bitterness, as they must have stared at Mother. "I said, 'Who else?' I said a lot of things, which as I say I disremember, and when I ran out of breath she did sidestep me. She just stepped around me and started walking off. Oh, I was fit to be tied, and I yelled at her, 'But you're her *mother!*' She missed a step then, just half a step, like a little piece left out of a motion picture, a little jerk, and then she went right on, and went back up to the house."

He moved to another bush and bent over it but didn't cut a blossom. "It was inhuman. It was—very peculiar. So I don't see that Kate has any cause to feel guilty. The talk around town was that she tried suicide a couple of times, on account of Kate's father. And when she did do it—all right, let's say it, when she shot herself—I don't think it was because Kate was going to marry me at all. I think it was because she was already unbalanced. I'm sorry, Althea, maybe I shouldn't say that to you—"

"Oh, don't mind me, darling. I think she was, too, and I knew her better than you did."

He turned to me. Once again he told me, "It's nice talking to you."

"Is it?" I was pleased. The sunny morning still affected me; I felt light as air.

"I can talk to you like a man."

I laughed. "I'm not sure I appreciate *that.*"

"Well, you know what I mean."

"Can't you talk to Kate about Mother?"

"Not any more. Of course, when her mother shot herself, Kate was all to pieces. We talked a lot then. After all, Kate was right there in the house when it happened—"

"I was, too."

"Well, after we got married Kate evidently decided to put the whole thing behind her, or bury it, and anyway, we . . . we had each other to think about."

A vision of their big double bed floated gently across my mind's eye. "Yes. Thank God." I said, "And Mother never did look at you?"

"Not if she could help it."

"That's interesting."

"Why?"

"Because it just occurred to me: in some ways you're a little bit like my father. Your size, your build, your—I don't know; you remind me of him vaguely."

He shrugged; he wouldn't accept the significance of that.

I was relieved. Anyone more Freud-oriented might have made something of it. I might have felt differently about him. Jack had given me a kind of psychic brush-off, however unintentional or unconscious. He was *not* going to represent my father, to me or anyone else. He wasn't going to be responsible for any complications of that nature. I wanted to laugh again; unreasoningly I felt the sunny innocent morning belonged to us, brother and sister, and but for that shrug it might not have.

Absent-mindedly he passed the roses from his nose to mine and dutifully I sniffed them. "As I told you before," he said, "your being here will do more to make Kate see things in the proper light than anything else. Well, I've taken enough of your time. I better be getting back, if you don't mind driving me in." But he stood a moment longer, gazing over the rose beds. And finally he said, as though echoing himself, "I ask you, what has Kate got to feel guilty about?"

It happened on the way to town, on the lake road to Stillbrook.

I know this road blindfold. I must have driven over it thousands of times. It has always belonged in a sense to the summer people and has changed very little in thirty years. Neat signs, embedded in the pine needles or hung from posts, identify the summer cottages: The Mastersons, Squirrels' Nest, On a Cove. . . . As children we often walked it, straggling along, stopping to throw stones at a rock that mysteriously rang, to examine a run-over snake, to drink whether thirsty or not from a little fern-lined spring. It isn't a memory-lined road, but it is the road of all my summers.

Shadow and sunlight fled over the car as Jack and I passed under the arch of trees, glimpses of blue lake flashed by, and the air was exhilarating with the scent of pine and stone and moss. Jack was driving the Ferrari again, and he was happy, too, in an intensely silent, set-faced way.

"Oh God, it's good to be alive!"

I said that. The words came up and out of me before I knew it. I said it.

Jack gave me a quick bright glance of agreement, and turned to the road again.

It was the joy, the unthinking, inadvertent joy that astounded me. The pointless joy, when I ask for nothing, expect nothing. *Joy:* unlovely word, calling to mind Salvation Army lasses, bluebirds of happiness, something always, until now, a little pathetic, a little synthetic. But this that I felt couldn't be described with any other word —a positive radiance breaking open in the heart, or spirit, some private unsuspected place, pushing out the incredible words in a golden burst.

What a mockery. It was good to be alive, I told myself, when we paused to drink from the spring, when a bleached down covered our arms and legs, and our eyes were as receptive, as empty, as unseeing and all-mirroring as pools of water. It was good to be alive even after the loss of innocence, on a summer night, coming home from a club dance in an open car with a beau, the moonlight flitting over our faces under this same tunnel of trees and the car radio playing sentimental night-club music from New York. . . .

But now! To have to say this, for the first time in my life, now!

I ground my teeth for an instant, and something like tears fought with disbelief, and then helpless, mystified, I quieted, held still within myself, awed.

Jack said at last, Yes, he always felt good in summer, too, the winters were very long here, in March everyone was fed up with it but you had two more months to go, if you were the kind that got depressed you sure did get depressed in March. . . . And then we turned down the main street of Stillbrook and pulled into the garage.

He hopped out, rested a hand on the door. "I enjoyed seeing you, Althea. Thanks for the roses. Take care, now." And holding his bouquet unselfconsciously, he crossed the pavement to the office.

I drove up Main Street to St. Michael's Church. I had no plan, but I had to communicate somehow that moment of joy, or find some way to measure it, or justify it, or explain it.

The church was empty. It breathed, as before, like a living body, but Father Bonneau wasn't there.

But coming out I saw down the road, beyond a hedge of evergreens, a white Victorian frame house with a parochial look to it, modernized with a great deal of gleaming, aluminum-framed plate glass, and situated in a rigidly neat, treeless lawn. I drove down, parked in the asphalt parking area, and rang the doorbell.

A black-moustached, black-uniformed woman, black hair caught back in a kerchief, came flying to the ornamented aluminum door and flung it open. "Yes!" she shouted. "Hallo! *Bonjour! Non!*" She waved her powerful arms, and you might have thought she was telling you to go away, the house was on fire, but I made out from a torrent of Canadian-accented French that it was indeed the rectory and although Father Bonneau was not in the house he was in the garden at the back. I thanked her and she quite impersonally slammed the door on me and went stampeding away again.

Coatless, wearing a faded blue butler's apron, Father Bonneau was peacefully painting garden chairs under an apple tree. He looked up as I approached and set his brush across the can of blue paint and straightened.

"Yes, you see," he said, as if continuing a conversation, "I find excuses to be away from my desk on a morning like this, when I should be answering a letter from the bishop. Come, we will sit down."

He drew two unpainted chairs, the heavy wooden kind with slanted back, into the shade of the apple tree and we seated ourselves. There was a grape arbor at the foot of the garden, and beyond this the mountains on the far side of the lake lifted their soft outlines.

Calmly Father Bonneau folded his hands. I was stricken with shyness then, a feeling of foolishness and religious inadequacy; once again in his presence I had become a child, sullen and awkward.

"They are martins," he said, and I realized I had been frowning at a kind of bird tenement high on a pole over the grape arbor; dark swallow-like birds, making a constant gratified burbling, streamed in and out of its doors and windows. "They come every year to the same house, and then in August they all go away again—to South America, I believe. That is amazing, isn't it? Year after year, to find their way back to this one birdhouse!" He shook his head, marveling, smiling with immense appreciation, the sunlight catching on his spectacles.

"It is touching," I said with a sense of despair.

"Oh no," he denied animatedly. "It is purely a matter of instinct. They cannot help themselves. There is no wish involved, or will, or trust, except as the innocence of doing what they must is trust."

"The absence of will is trust?"

"Ah yes, of course, among human beings. I was speaking of the birds, who have no choice. But then, you know, what choice do we have, in the long run, we human beings, except to do what we must—to grow, to find food, to keep warm in winter, to reproduce ourselves, to love God, to die?"

"We can choose not to love God," I said stubbornly.

"Oh, but we can't, you know, not really." He shook his head with indulgence. "Not really. The man who says, 'I cannot love God,' and in the next breath says, 'What a beautiful morning!' is contradicting himself."

I turned to look at this frail, grayish, whiskered face, almost to smile at the simplification, very affirmative and lucid and, as it were, sun-colored, that surrounded him like an atmosphere. Kitty with her time-sense would have understood him at once. Like taking up the language of a foreign land, one had only to accept Father Bonneau's point of view for everything to make perfect sense.

"Why," he commenced again suddenly, on the verge of laughter, "should people try not to love God? It must be such hard work! They must have to be on guard all the time. 'Yes, the sky is wonderful—but no, no, it is only a sky.' Only a sky! And in the end they sorrow that their lives seem to have no meaning. Why should they be afraid? It is so much more comfortable, loving God. Do they fear Him as they fear death, the unknown, the chaos of the unknown?"

He spread his hands. "Now you can see as well as I can that this beautiful morning is not an end but a beginning. It is order, the most exquisite order. Even the martins who have come all the way from South America to this house, even they play a little part in it. What is there to fear?" He folded his hands again, smiling. "It is not death, is it, but life. It is not unknown, or an idea, it is right here for us to see. It is real."

And I found myself looking into the answer, or an answer, once more, not fathoming it but mindlessly comprehending it, as I had done that night on Kitty's terrace. "Perhaps it's even more real than we are, this ordered God's world."

"Only if we choose not to believe in it."

"I've never chosen not to believe in it," I said thoughtfully. "But then, I've never chosen to believe in it either."

"And the time has come for you to decide?"

"I don't know." And I told him about my remarkable moment on the lake road.

He smiled. "Well then, you *are* deciding."

I was suddenly impatient with him. "I have no right to joy, Father!"

"Why? Because you are going to meet death soon? You said *God*, didn't you? You said, 'God, it is good to be alive'?"

"But did I *mean* God? Was I telling Him?"

"That is what you have to decide. If you had no right to joy how could you feel it?"

"Father," I said grimly, staring at the martin house, furious with my own clumsiness with his language, the language of church, spirit, and timelessness, "I have sinned all my life. Most of it. I have committed what you would call mortal sin."

"You would not call it that?"

"Yes," I said with a sigh. "Yes. I would call it that, too."

"You wish to atone for your sins?"

"I can't atone for them. There is no penance great enough."

"Who told you so?"

I turned to him, wanting to laugh. This wispy, whiskery man had toughness. I had had no intention, arriving here, of coming to grips with anything, certainly not of edging about the word "God"; yet without persuasion he was forcing me in spite of myself to look at the undecipherable answer. There seemed no way of shying away from anything, with him. Zebstrow, when I shied, made a little note with his pencil and let it pass. Father Bonneau, less sophisticated, innocent of techniques, seemed to prod me along the path I had unwittingly stumbled into.

I got to my feet.

"Perhaps," said Father Bonneau softly, rising also, "you began your penance this morning."

"With joy, Father?" I asked incredulously.

"With loving life," he answered.

7

The Goodfellows' mill is deep in the woods, and their Sunday lunch turned out to be a large, sprawling party under the trees.

I gather this is the present-day in-group of Stillbrook. Attractive, most of them youngish, they roamed up and down the stone steps or sat on the lower terrace in the shade, while the stream fell with a long constant sigh and the great wheel turned ponderously. They are what Sarah Hodge calls "come-heres"—exurbanites who have taken up permanent residence in the country, and, like Simon and Margo, participate in civic affairs, sit on school and hospital boards, run for local office.

A far cry from the old-time city people, who were never more than summer visitors. There were just two groups in Stillbrook then—the summer visitors and, as we called them, the natives, and although we respected each other we often privately laughed at each other.

I can see us, the younger summer crowd, drawn up in our big cars, which would be considered very square today, waiting in front of the old cramped post office for the noon mail to be sorted, smothering giggles at the local shapes and costumes passing before us, for Stillbrook seemed inhabited entirely by eccentrics then; or eating scrambled eggs at Austin's, the all-night diner on Railroad Avenue, polo coats over our bias-cut chiffon evening dresses, ignoring the stares of the town riff-raff—how *dégagê* we were, or thought we were, sleek and insular! How simple and frivolous and naïve life was, and how much we had to learn and unlearn! Our elders had chosen to avoid the snobbery of more fashionable resorts, but our obvious uniqueness in Stillbrook, the uniqueness of Stillbrook itself, a place our city friends had never heard of, made minor-league snobs of us after all, like initiates in a cult.

And then after Labor Day, full of heady plans for football weekends, tea dances, coming-out parties, we were gone.

It seems a hundred years ago. The teen-agers of today don't play for two months, as we did, but earnestly look for summer jobs. The little rickety golf club where we danced on Saturday night in our chiffon dresses has been spruced up and is open to the public. The post office, even, has been replaced by a brick Georgian edifice with a mural—deemed appropriate to a New England village by Olympian architects. Are there tea dances any more? Certainly the glamor of the cities has vanished. The natives have had the last laugh.

And from the look of the countryside, the dissolution of farming, the pastures growing over, the mushrooming rambler-ranch-types, trailers, motels, even estate developments, one might say the old-time natives, too, are a past entity.

"But why," demanded Ginny Clay during lunch, her jaw rounded, "should anyone want an area to remain backward, fifty years behind the times, merely for the sake of picturesqueness?" And her husband, perhaps sensing a dispute in the offing, gave her a wary glance.

"Never was good farming land," Jack remarked mildly. "Barely scratch a living out of it. I sometimes wonder how the folks on my place ever managed, especially in winter."

"Peace and quietness," suggested Kitty, almost in a whisper, with soft, far-seeing eyes.

"Cold privies," countered Margo, on a ludicrous warbling note.

We were gathered in a circle on the lower terrace. A buffet had been arranged on the upper one outside the millhouse, and the guests sat at little tables on both levels or perched decoratively on stone steps and walls. A stout Swiss girl had brought out the Goodfellows' two self-contained children, a boy and girl of four and six, to be presented to the company and then removed. I had discovered myself to be guest of honor; once again I was being launched. Kitty had gracefully taken charge of introductions, and Simon, infatuation-prone, clung meditatively to my side. Rob Clay gave me a professional once-over from a distance, but when Ginny joined us with her plate he followed in her footsteps.

Simon roused himself to utter a pronouncement. "It

was not peaceful," he said, whistling *s*'s through his long teeth, "so much as simple. And it wasn't quiet so much as austere. There were no complexities and no conveniences. It was a time of absolutes: labor or privation, drought or rainfall, sickness or health, life or death. You have only to look at the family graveyards of the eighteen-hundreds—infants, children under three, and some old codger surrounded by the two or three wives he wore out along the way. Diphtheria, consumption—am I right, Rob? No, we should not mourn the good old days."

"That's just what I was saying," claimed Ginny inaccurately, gesturing broadly and spilling wine. "I'm really sick of all this looking back. Progress is progress. Better schools, better health, better living conditions. Maybe it is materialism, but let's face it, we do not live in a romantic age any more. It's pretty shoddy to idealize peace and quietness when people all over the world are going hungry and the H-bomb hangs over our heads." She darted a little glare at me. "After all, what are wars made of? I must say—"

I watched her as she rambled on. Her diatribe was for some reason aimed not at Kitty but at me, although I hadn't opened my mouth. Ginny Clay, young, healthy, attractive, resented me. I couldn't imagine why. I was amused.

Temperately Rob put in, "Of course, with the betterment of living standards you get an increase in population, and with a population explosion you inevitably get a breakdown of moral standards."

"Oh good God," said Ginny to the company at large, "we were *not* talking about moral standards. And anyway, equating the betterment of human society with a breakdown of moral standards is the most insidious rot of all. This is the kind of reactionary talk that gives the Left a platform—"

She must be, I thought, a practiced spokesman at PTA meetings, Town Meeting, the League of Women Voters. As before, the company seemed unwilling to take her belligerence seriously. Rob went on eating without change of color or expression as if he were used to being publicly doused, so to speak, with cold water.

"It's a platform," said Simon, "older than anything called Left: organized society versus the individual."

"Oh no, Simon," Ginny told him, "you're *way* off the track—"

"Progress versus peace and quietness," Kitty offered again, in a murmur.

"Down with people!" Margo laughed, throwing up her hands in abandon.

"I didn't mean," Rob began again, "to equate progress with degeneration, but we did use the word materialism—"

"*I* used it," Ginny interrupted him patiently, "in a purely hypothetical sense. You see," she explained to us, "he is an idealist, a hopeless premise in any serious discussion of contemporary problems. Now, the point I've been *trying* to make. . . ."

I glanced at Jack, who, head bowed, was staring down into his empty plate. Kitty looked like a child among grown-ups, her eyes large and dubious, foreswearing mirth as the better part of caution. It had become one of those moments when there seemed no way out of a clash with real unpleasantness.

"My God, the coffee!" cried Margo, leaping to her feet and scattering contention like an impulsive dinner guest tipping over the tableware. "Everybody's finished and I forgot to make coffee! Rob, be a lamb, will you, and bring the plates? Althea, you haven't been inside the house. Would you like to see it?"

Ginny, checked, sat open-mouthed in midsentence for a moment, pugnacity draining from her face. "Can I help you, Margo?" she asked quite humbly, as we began to move away.

"No, dear, stay and talk to Simon! Tell her about this week's editorial, Simon. I think Ginny would appreciate it." Margo went warbling and pealing ahead of us, and I smiled at her blatant ingenuity.

The house was indeed out of the ordinary. We stood in a barn-like room. "It's mostly Shaker," said Margo vaguely, indicating the sparse furniture, and it was Margo who had painted the large energetic abstractions lurking in the raftered upper reaches. Concealed speakers were quietly playing Bartok, and the plain, polished spaces smelled of wax and ancient chaff.

How different from Kitty's womb-like house. I couldn't imagine sitting down cozily to sew, for example, in Margo's barren living room—if you could call it that—for it was only sketchily partitioned from the rest of the building, but it was a good place to study Zen, or read Kafka, or practice Yoga. In winter, I thought, the wind would sigh and the great rafters would creak, and unlike Kitty's house the bygone voices of families, the lingering exhalations of love and sorrow, would be missing; it was antidomestic. Yet it had a special stimulating atmosphere of its own, something that coolly appealed to the mind rather than the psyche, and lifted one refreshingly into a quickened, expanded sphere of cerebration. I had to revise my impression of Margo then, the earthy Toulouse-Lautrec music-hall girl, and replace her against this existential background, and I was thankful that Kitty, mystical, diffident, dependent, had such a friend.

I expressed my thankfulness to Margo.

"Anyone who has Kate for a friend," Margo replied unequivocally, "can consider themselves fortunate." Rob had disappeared into the kitchen area with the plates and we could hear the tap running. "She's a *rara avis*, isn't she? Not too many people show so much of their souls." Margo frowned, searching for words. "She sensitizes."

I smiled. "She does."

"She does it to all of us. Ginny, for instance, is genuinely fond of Kate." She added with a twist of her penciled eyebrows, "And Ginny's good will is pretty powerful stuff." In spite of herself Margo gave way to a laugh that climbed in little arcs into the rafters. She sobered. "I think we'd almost rather see Kate happy than be happy ourselves."

"I know the feeling."

She regarded me levelly. Her guests were streaming

in now, bearing more plates. She said, "And some day I hope we do see her happy; really happy." She went off with her guests to the kitchen area, where there was now considerable confusion.

Sunlight poured down a gleaming corridor from a half-open Dutch door. Drawn to it, I discovered a kind of balcony over the falls. I stepped out, and a moment later Rob Clay wandered out, too, and we leaned our elbows on the railing and put our faces gratefully to the water-ruffled air. The cascade beneath us was too noisy for us to communicate without shouting, but neither of us wanted to make conversation. The rush of water, the fern-scented vapor, purged our brains, clarified our senses, our eyes and ears and nostrils, and when at last we moved we were both smiling a private smile.

Rob indicated the wooden walkway, or bridge, and we went down some steps and across the stream to the opposite bank. A path carpeted with pine needles led away from the stream, and we followed it up a rise and came out at length on a knoll in full sunlight, crowned with an immense boulder and a little grove of white birches. From here the land fell away to a distant valley and undulated on to the dim, placid mass of the great mountains to the north.

"This is far enough," said Rob, placing a hand on the boulder. "Let's sit down a minute."

"I'm not tired."

"Let's sit down."

"There is something so adamant about you."

"It's the Scot in me."

We sat with our backs to the boulder and crossed our ankles. He asked me impersonally how I was feeling and I told him remarkably well on the whole, and he nodded as if in consent. When I looked him in the face he glanced away at the view, and when I turned to the view he studied me obliquely. We were shy in this setting, stretched out like strangers in adjacent deck chairs on an ocean voyage. We kept silent again for a while, with much, or perhaps at that moment very little, to occupy our thoughts, for the clear sun-drenched air was somewhat stupefying.

"Do you have a cigarette?"

"I don't smoke," he told me. "You shouldn't either."

"My God, Rob," I sighed, shaking my head at him, "do you think it matters?" and he caught his lip in his teeth for an instant, frowning, chagrined.

"I say that to everyone," he explained.

"I'll bet you do. I'll bet you make life miserable—" I stopped and rubbed my forehead with both hands.

He was so quiet that I turned to look at him, and he turned to me—faintly, rather bleakly, smiling—and I saw in his eyes the unsatisfactory part of his life, or at least the depth of indomitable endeavor, the quest not for happiness but for goodness, for some equation, and I pitied and loved him, and smiled with him. Seven children, I thought wearyingly, not one of which he loves the less because he cannot lose himself in them. And Ginny. A lonely man.

We were gazing at the view again. "I feel," I said, not knowing what I was going to say, not intending anything pretentious, almost in the kind of free association Zebstrow kept trying vainly to lull me into; but moved, moved without will, to say it, "I feel as if you and I have a great sense of mercy at this moment."

The air pulsated with light and breeze.

"Mercy," he said quietly at last. "That's a word one doesn't hear very often. Compassion; pity. But mercy . . ."

"Let go, Rob. You don't have to balk so with me. You know what I mean. Yes, mercy."

He gave a little sigh. "Yes." He compressed his lips, his orange eyebrows knitted. "There is a sense of mercy in the air here, isn't there?"

"Not in the air. In us. It began over the stream."

"Yes." He spoke as if groping his way in strange territory. "I was aware of it. It took away our shells. It left us with this—with nothing else but this feeling of mercy."

"That's it," I breathed.

Rob folded his arms and we held perfectly still in the indulgent sunlight. He said, "It's an odd word for you to use. I wouldn't have thought you knew the meaning of it. I thought you took dying much too lightly, and dying can be a very majestic thing. I thought you had probably gone through life taking everything too lightly, or trying to."

"Well, I did."

"I would have thought you knew much better the meaning of things like bitterness or regret or fighting back. But mercy. That's rather majestic in itself."

"Yes, it is. It's new to me. A great deal is new to me."

He unfolded his arms and took my hand, manipulated it as if testing its bones and tendons, its fragility. He said, "This is new to me, too." He meant, this moment, this feeling, this pervading beneficence. There was a sadness in his pensive kneading. I took his chin and turned it and pressed my lips lightly to his. I saw his blue eyes widen, astonished and a little fearful.

I smiled, drawing back. "You are good, Robert. You *are* good. You ought to accept that." I was getting to my feet, and he stood up also, dusting pine needles from his trousers. "You're needed, not because you're a medicine man but because you're a good man. That's not to be minimized."

"Althea," he said, reprovingly, reaching for me, and we held each other for a moment, not really knowing why, or what, if anything, to do about it. And the fire, the old fire, threatened to break open in me, even while I felt it threatening to in him, the breath catching in his throat. But mercy, the sense of merciful love, was stronger still, held us still, cradled us, soothed us, smiled on us.

I moved apart from him and he didn't try to keep me. I slipped an arm through his. "Come on, darling. We can't really improve on a moment like this, can we? Let's go back."

It is midsummer. I haven't felt like writing, for writing means thinking. I live precariously between two poles, peace and dread.

I awake each morning with the sense of being newborn. Just for a moment, while my eyes open to the sunlight sparkling at the windows and I become aware of the stillness, the fragrance—I am new, innocent! I lie without moving and there is a distillation of harmony in my cool, quiet room, and I am once again the vessel, the focal point, for joy, and I breathe from the soul, "Thank God!" out loud, smiling. To what, to whom? To summer? To Father Bonneau's over-all Order?

And then something trembles, unresolved, like thunderheads massed silently on the horizon, something waits in the distance, and I have to tell my deluded self that I am not innocent, that I am old, old with the weight of sins and the seeds of death, and I sigh, sit up, ring for Bernice. Sometimes this doesn't happen immediately, and I linger tranquilly over my breakfast tray with its pink rose or red (never white, please, I told Bernice), holding the spell unbroken, but the sigh comes up involuntarily, sooner or later. I have no right, in spite of Father Bonneau's quasidispensation, to joy.

Then I alternate between days of restlessness and days of inertia, flight and surrender, the two poles.

The lake and its shores are reaching a peak of summertime activity, the great play time. The droning of boats never ceases until long after dark. Water skiers, knees and buttocks ardently protruding, cross one's wearied view from left to right and right to left. At the golf club men and women in Bermuda shorts track their way over the greens in the afternoon haze, their faces brooding with a strange, reluctant compulsion, and from behind the club house comes the determined *clop* . . . *clop* of a tennis rally. Cocktail party invitations arrive in every mail (now that I have been introduced to the in-group)—dachshunds with pretzels strung on their tails, martini glasses unaccountably emitting bubbles, roosters, balloons, one harried card with no name on it at all.

I take the car and go far afield on back roads, past deserted farms and pastures and stone walls, where the very sunbaked granite, and the grass, smell of a simpler era; up into mountainy woods of pine and white birch, fern-carpeted, parklands of solitude where everything is exactly as the seasons have left it, a world of apparent stillness, yet filled with a minutiae of sound—leaves sighing against the sky, the whispers of the eternal moment-to-moment growth and decay of vegetation, a bird deep in the musky shadows, pensively practicing long flute-like notes, each slow arpeggio ending in query . . .

I stop the car and get out and pluck a leaf, one pale

clean young leaf, and examine it closely, the intricacy and symmetry of its veins, its velvet texture, its eloquent muteness. And it is suddenly a tragedy that I don't know the name of the tree this leaf belongs to, and the names of many other trees, and will never know, that it is too late to study the microcosmic miracle of leaves. Such a little thing to know, yet suddenly so profoundly, so agonizingly, important.

A church fair is taking place in a remote village. The booths of home-baked food, white elephants, and so on, are set up in the stalls of the old carriage shed, and the little crowd mills about in the heat and light reflected from the side of the white frame church. I stop again and buy a paper cup of emerald-green lemonade and a second-hand book of stories by Sarah Orne Jewett, and I am smiled on by spirited church-workers. And I think with an almost overpowering tenderness, This is beautiful, this is magical! Even the little book, bound in white with a decoration of green vines, seems to claim me, and I feel it is meant for me; I was destined to buy it. A child's smokey eyes, her flush and silent acceptance when I offer to treat her to the green lemonade, send me into transports of gratitude.

In this same mood of restlessness I go to a random cocktail party and look at the pink and lavender dresses and the inclined male heads and the anxieties and needs and blameless frivolities. I leave in half an hour. I rise in the night to walk barefoot on the wet grass. The sky shimmers with stars, stock and nicotiana release their scents in the privacy of darkness, and out on the quiet water loons break into abrupt laughter, the primeval chuckles and wails that must have echoed over the empty lake in Kitty's Indian wilderness. The night, too, opens its secrets to me.

I am in love with the immaterial, heretofore invisible and inaudible, detail of life, the tiny insubstantial graces. The past and the nonfuture no longer enthrall me, and I am ravenous for the present moment, the seconds of each day; and every hour with its revelations is a lifetime.

Then exhaustion suddenly takes possession of me, and I lie all day on the dock, scarcely moving. I breathe the skeletonized odor of dock wood in a stillness of mind as well as body, and I sleep. I embrace oblivion.

Yesterday my own voice woke me, crying, "Murph!" I lay stunned, gazing with my face turned on my cheek at the dark-green shingles of the boathouse, reviewing the facts like a patient in the first shocked, stupefied coming-to from an anaesthetic. . . . He had been with me again, upstairs in the boathouse. We lay sealed together, arms and thighs interlocked, his dark perspiring brow wedged against mine, our bodies convulsing in the final volcanic moments of passion. . . .

More than twenty years ago, I told myself. The days when appetites and passion were possible for me, I told myself, are over. The fire, which I had all but forgotten until the afternoon of Margo's luncheon party, is out. I lay trying to get this through my head, memorizing it. What a bad joke, this dream! My body, my spirit, threaten to come awake, and it is too late.

And when the sun and fire and despair become intolerable I slide into the water, the rapturous cool water, enfolding me in its forgiveness, and I move in it for a long time, turning and floating and burrowing, until the torment breaks apart in me with a dry sobbing, and for a little while I am free, barrenly at peace once more, and I climb out and sleep again. . . .

This, I tell myself, is what I get for coming back to Northwater.

My mother, when she died, could not have suffered pain. Oblivion must have come in a single explosion. Did she ever really suffer at all in her life? Does madness preclude suffering? Did she revenge herself on life with the suffering of others?

But last night, a still more harrowing apparition. Restless again, I went to my window and looked down into Mother's rose garden, and she was there. Bending, pausing as if listening, moving on again, from bush to bush. . . .

I held my breath, digging my nails into my cheeks, telling myself in a silent scream, You're running a temperature, you know that, it's the fever, you're dreaming again! But I was actually ready to leap back in case she looked up at me, although I had the terrible feeling she knew I was there all the time.

Fury broke over me in a perspiration. I ran down the hall in my bare feet, my thin gown streaming behind me, down the great staircase past the mute pipes and the glowering tusks and all the glass eyes, and over the fur and the hides and the cool floor and out across the veranda. . . .

No one was there. She was gone. I stood under the trellis, my lungs creaking. "All right!" I cried. (Did I really cry this into the night, out loud, across the rose garden, or was I dreaming still?) "I suffer! If you want me to suffer I do suffer! Have done with us!"

Oh God, is my mind going now, with my body? Is this part of her revenge?

At any rate, Rob came today. Perhaps he has some private agreement with Bernice, and she sent for him; I couldn't bear to ask. He told me on his last visit that he would drop in from time to time to see how I was getting on, and I let it go at that.

He found me in the library, the coolest, darkest room in the house. The furniture is teakwood, and there are lacquered chests and sandalwood Buddhas, and one can imagine one's self to be in a rather posh opium den. In my bathing suit and white robe I was sitting at the big desk sorting out bills and correspondence before going down to the dock. The Tiffany lamp was turned on.

Rob strode in looking hot and tired and on the verge of being irritable. Perhaps he had done some serious thinking since that Sunday; he hadn't intended to get on a personal footing with me, and as a professional man he would not be taken advantage of. Ah me. His red hair gleamed, he frowned and did not smile. He sat down beside the desk and reached for my wrist, murmuring,

"How're you doing, Althea?" and concentrated over his watch.

I smiled, even if he did not. My eyes smarted inexplicably. Once again I wished to reassure him. And the pressure of his fingers on my wrist sent a current to the core of me, producing an astonished, exasperated sigh, and a kind of laughing despondency filled me, and then a harshness, the opposite of mercy, and with an angry effort of will I tried to lock myself off from him.

"I'm doing all right," I told him, bored with sickness, pain, torment.

He dropped my wrist and raised his eyes and studied my face thoughtfully. He had got sunburnt since the last time I saw him and the bridge of his nose had peeled, and there were flakes of skin over his bleached eyebrows. Where have you been, I wanted to ask him, what have you been doing? Did you take the children to the beach in Maine, were you trapped in someone's open boat?

He let go of my wrist and asked it of me: "What have you been doing?"

I sat far back in my chair, away from him, my arms folded. "Why? Am I worse or better?"

He declined to answer that, pursing his lips. "What have you been doing?"

"Rob, does it matter? Sometimes I take it easy, sometimes I go at full tilt." And without warning to myself I put my head down on my arms on the desk. Peace, peace, I cried, dry-eyed.

His hand rested on my sleeved upper arm. "Have you been taking your medication?"

I straightened and sat, chin in hand, looking away to the lake beyond the windows. "Yes, I've been taking it."

"Sleeping at night?"

I glanced at him guardedly. "Fairly well."

"All right. I'm going to change your prescription." He had reached in his breast pocket and was scribbling on a pad. He tore off a sheet. "Now, I want you to come to my office for some more tests."

"But I told you—"

"I'm telling you, Althea. If I'm going to be your physician you will have to do as I ask." We stared at each other.

"When?"

"This afternoon."

I smiled, finally. "All right." And at that, involuntarily, my eyes did fill with tears.

He took my hand, as he had done that Sunday, but now he let it lie across his palm, and contemplated it. Then he looked up and shook his head at me. For a half-second the starved sadness stood in his eyes. "Don't go at full tilt any more, Althea." Carefully he clasped my hand and returned it to the desk. He got up and moved away. "I'll see you in my office."

I sat turning the pages of a magazine in the waiting room with an old man and two shapeless women, country people. Their garments, their hair and faces, seemed faded, unpressed, while I, at first, felt uniquely sleek in Chinese silk. The feeling made me vaguely uncomfortable. It wasn't due to our relative status, I realized; it had something to do with doctors' waiting rooms, where the light is dim, an electric fan stirs the stale, fateful air, the pages of magazines rustle wearily.

I thought about this while I sat there. It was their patience, their older, wiser acceptance of mortality, that blurred these people for me, and it was my own impatience, my fear, my inexperience, my paradoxical newness to life, that made me feel naïvely sleek and clean. They had been born to this faded, nobler philosophy of life's inevitable defeat without ever having had to acquire it, while I was learning it against my will, considering it punishment. I was sure that were I to fall down ignominiously in a fit they would move with calm humanity to help me. I sensed this in the way they looked into my face once, smiled, and went back to their magazines or their vacant-eyed thoughts, as if they knew me better than I knew myself; whereas if one of them had succumbed I would have screamed in a panic for the doctor. They waited, in this waiting room; I sat tensed, self-conscious, resentful.

Inside in the examining room a young woman chattered in a high carefree voice, the words indistinguishable, and Rob murmured in answer, and then a baby suddenly shrieked in outrage, perhaps at a needle; its mother chatted on imperturbably over the shrieks and at length the baby subsided heartbrokenly—never, never again to trust humankind in the same way, and quieted at last to grieving hiccoughs.

Through the walls of the other side of the house came the sound of a brief commotion—children running upstairs, pounding pell-mell down again. A car door slammed in the driveway, and I turned to the window to see Ginny at the wheel of a station wagon filled with children; she glanced over her shoulder at them distractedly and uttered a warning word or two, and they snapped the door locks and settled down, and then they drove away. A strange jealous pity filled me at sight of those tender necks and ears and the gradations of red hair, from pale gold through pink to auburn; I felt a jealous compassion even for Ginny's dutiful glance over her shoulder, her young face blankly inured to the harassments of motherhood.

Rob was ushering out the chatty woman with the baby; he spied me and beckoned. He wore a white jacket, and here in his office he was more friendly in a business-like way.

When he was through with me and I was leaving he asked suddenly, writing at his desk, "Are you depressed, Althea?"

"Why?" I answered, turning. "Can you give me a pill to make me happy?"

He looked up. He considered my irony, decided not to respond to it. "I can give you an antidepressant."

I wanted to laugh. Then I, too, answered gravely, "You said dying could be majestic. Let me try it without fakery." I stopped. I felt the blood drain from my cheeks, and I asked the question I hadn't asked since Zurich. All the arrogance left my voice. "How soon, Rob? How soon will it be, do you think?"

"I don't know," he said at last. His eyes told me, I am

helpless; at the same time they told me, I will do all in my power to help you.

There was nothing more to say. For an instant I longed to be held in his arms again, comforted, but in a sense the unwavering solemnity of his eyes did this for me.

I opened the door, went out, closed it quietly. The shapeless faces in the waiting room lifted to watch me go.

I found myself heading for Kitty's hilltop.

In the throes of the pole-to-pole contest, the waxing and waning like the pain and ecstasy of birth, I hadn't so much avoided Kitty as left her out. I was possessed, powerless. Now, sobered by Rob and his waiting room, my need for Kitty, her need for me—they were almost the same thing—awoke again, and it was only natural to turn in her direction.

I wasn't expected, of course, and for a moment, arriving quietly on the hilltop, I felt as if I had come unobserved upon the intimate, habitual communion of this little black house with its open-pastured setting. The afternoon was cloudy, and here the gray sky was close to the earth, and the house, with no sign of human life about, actually looked as if it were engaged in some inaudible colloquy with tree, sky, and fields. It had been there so long, so many families had lived there, children in long dresses, bearded patriarchs, women in sunbonnets, and their animals with them, dogs and cattle and cats, they had all come and gone, and the huddled weathered wood and opalescent glass and bricks were saturated with content, energy, and now in its silence the old house breathed a brooding life of its own.

Oh, Carlo Branzini, would you take back that remark about my unseeing eyes? And what would be the labyrinthine judgment of Herr Doktor Zebstrow? Is this belated extra-dimensional sight customary with the dying? Or is it morbid, part of the malignancy, pointing the way to hallucinations such as the one of Mother in the rose garden? And yet I give way to it with delight and wonder, as I did to the child at the church fair and the book and the leaf, as if it were a first and last approach to wisdom, the final lifting of veils, and I see, I see, and all is freshness, and the world I have never seen before enchants me.

I didn't call out to Kate but went quietly in at the kitchen door. The communing mood prevailed; I felt that she was communing too.

Yes, she was sitting on the terrace; no book in her lap, no sewing—just sitting there, alone, her head bowed, her hands loosely clasped in her lap. I could see the little ladder of vertebrae going up the back of her neck, and tears sprang to my eyes.

My sister, my sister, what troubles you, what weighs on you so heavily?

I tiptoed back to the kitchen, opened and shut the screen door and called, "Hi, Kitty!" We met then in the shadowy parlor and I put my arms around her. Her face, in the brief glimpse before I embraced her, was drained of color. Even her dark eyes seemed blanched.

"Kitty, what have I done to you?"

She drew back, astonished. "Done to me, Althea?"

"Shall I go away again? Close Northwater for good?"

She clutched my arms. "No, don't. Please don't."

The fury welled up in me. "She threatened to kill you, don't you remember that? She said she would kill you and then herself if you went off with Jack! She always bordered on the psychotic but she went right out of her head those last few weeks. Everybody knew it. You could hear her all over the house when she gave way to those tirades. How can you blame yourself? Why can't you be grateful that she set you free?"

I could have gone on. There was much more of this buried fury than I realized, but commiseration had appeared again in my sister's eyes. She was almost smiling, and I found it was I, now, who was clutching her. My grip loosened, and she said, "Althea, I'm not trying to punish myself, but let me be ungrateful if I want to be."

I stared at her. "I've never heard you say anything so sardonic."

"I didn't mean it to be. I grieve over what happened and you mustn't try to prevent me. I was able to shut it out of my mind for a long time and that was a mistake. I must get over it, yes, but in my own time." She did smile, faintly. "You were angry. It's odd about your anger. It makes me feel better."

I shook my head. "You are a puzzle. How stubborn you are about your penitence. Of the two of us I would have said I was the more cool-headed, but now I'm not so sure."

"I know. I don't understand it. Jack is the only one who understands me, and yet he couldn't tell you in words what he understands." Her eyebrows slanted together in sympathy for Jack, and for herself, and she laughed. "Do you ever think how mysterious it is to be yourself?"

It was a startling question, however ingenuous, but I laughed, too, and gave her a farewell hug, and then I found myself answering her in silence. To know you are dying and at the same time feel you are being reborn? Yes, how mysterious!

And again the waiting distance trembled, the sense of some inevitable expiation, and for an instant I stared over Kitty's shoulder at the long view through the open door, and held my breath.

9

I bestirred myself while this remission, as Rob called it, lasted, and decided to repay some of my social obligations. A perfectly normal gesture, and yet even as I lifted the phone I felt inescapably hinged to the abnormal, and wondered if I was capable of carrying off so simple a thing as a supper party for six without catastrophe.

I invited Kitty and Jack and the Goodfellows, and, daringly, Father Bonneau. I didn't know how the others would take to the priest or even if he would accept my invitation, but he said over the phone without surprise, "Yes, how kind of you," the words warmed with a smile.

I was reminded of the old days in Rome, the last time I had played at hostess, when there was almost always a representative of the Church at table. I had in truth played at hostess, for Branzini did the inviting so casually and we entertained so constantly, if only the handful of Branzini relatives staying in the house at the time, that dinners for ten to twenty were a matter of course. The seasoned staff needed little direction, and I merely occupied one end of the table.

Branzini even told me what to wear, the first year or two, and I accepted this willingly also, for he had gone to the couturiers with me and ordered costumes I scarcely had the nerve to wear of my own choice—Borgia-like robes of velvet and fur, Grecian draperies clasped with vine leaves, sumptuously embroidered saris, and all curiously sinister, not because of their suggestive slits and décolletages and transparencies but because these details contributed to an effect of formal, counterfeit sexuality. I felt in Branzini's costumes like one of those brittle, unapproachable women, rigged out to be seductive, bosom precariously exposed, in the Comédie Française—not only unapproachable but cynically irreproachable.

Even so, the churchly representatives at dinner kept their eyes averted from me.

And night after night I sat at the end of that rococo table, staring through branches of gilded epergnes and candelabra over a welter of crested goblets, down the rows of faces like the reduplicated posters on an Italian highway, and so bored I became, so maddened with entrapment, with Branzini's hauteur—his care not to look at me until it was time to rise, with his relatives' patronizing civility and the gorgeous flattery of would-be lovers, that no one knew the difference when I took to drugs.

How wasteful of me, rather than take a lover! Zebstrow called it retaliation: "He expected you to be unfaithful in recognition of his indifference. Taking drugs was the real infidelity." But Branzini wouldn't believe I had been faithful; it made him laugh. It makes me laugh now. For it wasn't retaliation, and I was almost too embarrassed to tell Zebstrow what it was. After all the untidy experimentation of my youth, the amateurish lending of the body, the frivolity of an early elopement, there existed deep within me some Puritan bloom, lonely as a daffodil, some slender pitiful longing for rectitude. The chagrin of that first marriage and Mother's high-handed contrivance of an annulment smarted still, and I was determined to respect the contract of this second marriage and make it last. I could at least, if it was too late to be wifely, be faithful.

("But you had tried to be faithful once before, had you not?" remarked Zebstrow, gazing out the window like a battered, zoo-weary lion. "To your papa?")

The chaste little plant perished, of course. Unwittingly I had dedicated myself to being a possession, the thing Branzini most wanted, and his interest, attenuated as it was by forced refinements and gratifications, was bound to wane. And at last I joined in the destruction, ground the little plant to earth even after it was extinct, and the drugs, the long separations from Branzini and the final one, the increasingly gaudy life, the overdue collapse, brought me to Zurich and Zebstrow, and finally we discovered I was diseased beyond recovery anyway. A dismal record.

In full circle I was back at Northwater.

But whether as a result of that purely ornamental participation at my own table, or the sense of approaching calamity, I found myself in a tremble over this little supper party, and I was relieved when Bernice took over. "Leave all to me," she said in her enameled French, expanding visibly like a bird lifting its plumage. "Ah, but how I have despaired that we might exercise the hospitality! Be tranquil. All will be perfect." And she marched off to make lists, examine china, browbeat the glum and docile Helga.

Coming down the morning of the party, I heard sounds in Mother's little sink room off the conservatory. The tap was running; someone was arranging flowers. I froze. Another hallucination? But it was Sarah Hodge, I found, filling the tall tin holding-vessels with lilies and delphinium and stock, relayed to her by Clarence. We exchanged good mornings, and I leaned, a little dizzy with relief, against a twisted Moorish pillar.

The conservatory, an octagonal room tiled in purple and green mosaic, contains a wall fountain that drips like a leaky faucet into a pool in the floor. Tall windows embroidered with stained-glass water lilies let in the light. I can remember when it was filled with gardenias and camellias, miniature orange trees, orchids, ferns, potted palms—an exotic little jungle manufacturing its own heady humidity. It is empty of plant life now, but someone thought to turn on the fountain when I returned, and the slow cryptic dripping echoes metallically against the bare tiles.

"I wish yaw *mothah* could see you now." Once again Sarah burst out with praise. "You *nevah* looked so well even in them days."

Involuntarily my hand lifted to touch my cheek. "Is that really so, Sarah?"

"Ayah, it's so. Need to put on more flesh, of course, but well, yaw *mothah* always called you beautiful, and if you'll forgive my saying so I couldn't rightly agree with her. Oh, you was pretty, right enough, mebbe al*most* beautiful, but beauty isn't all in looks, is it? Wa'n't much happiness in your face, nor character, them days. All I can say is, I wish she could see you now."

I in turn studied Sarah as she stood by the copper sink, her puffy bleached hands poised over the grouped stalks, her white hair and white uniform immaculate as snow. "You were very fond of her, weren't you, Sarah?"

But something slid evasively like a tiny silver fish across her moist pale eyes. "Well, now thy-ah, poor thing. I did my best for her, and I hope she was satisfied."

It wasn't an answer, I knew, but I pressed on. "You were in the house the day she died, weren't you?"

Her breath rushed inwardly through her porcelain teeth. "Ayah, I was."

"In fact, you were the first to reach her."

Her hands fell to the rim of the sink and she bowed her head. "I don't like to think of it."

"Yes, I remember. We heard the gun go off, and I came to the door of my sitting room, and you ran past me to her bedroom."

"Poor woman. Poor, poor woman."

"You must have heard the quarrel with Kitty beforehand."

"Ayah." Sarah couldn't ask me to drop the subject, but her eyes turned to me imploringly. "I wa'n't eavesdropping, mind, but I was down on the stay-ahs, polishing them brass *rawds* that hold the ca'pet down, and, well, when yaw mothah had the *hy*-sterics it wa'n't no use trying to shut your *e*-ahs."

She looked at me, hoping she needn't go on, but I waited, and with a little groan she continued.

"When she got through it was quiet, real quiet. Katherine went to her room and shut the door, I heard that, and I said to myself, Now thy-ah, it's all over, and I hope Katherine don't pay no mind to what she said, she didn't mean it. She couldn't kill nobody, least of all her own daughter, and she ain't going to kill herself this time no more 'n any of the other times. So it was quiet for mebbe three-four minutes, and then—well, then—there was that terrible noise. Terrible. Seemed like I wanted to disbelieve it, seemed like I stayed there on my knees hoping suthin' would take the sound out o' my head like, but nothing did, and finally I got to my feet and sta'ted scrambling up the stay-ahs—" Sarah's eyes sprinkled little tears over her cheeks, and she shook her head and fumbled in her apron for a handkerchief, and vigorously wiped her eyes with sideways strokes.

"Kitty had opened the door opposite mine," I mused, taking up where Sarah left off, "and we stood there staring at each other after you ran past, and then we started down the hall after you, but you came out of Mother's room and told us not to go in."

I had forgotten that moment when we stared at each

other across the hall, the horror in Kitty's eyes paralyzing me, and my horror paralyzing her, and the moment seemed to go on and on and we couldn't seem to bring an end to it. I was realizing now that those minutes before and after the shot were out of all proportion to actual time, some of them compressed into seconds and others protracted into endless, motionless intervals.

Sarah was stripping leaves from the lower stalks of the lilies. "Ayah, she finally did it, poor thing. Old Doctor Clay come, and Tom Preston, and I told them what I told you, and that's all there was to it." Sarah gave a final sniffle. "And may she rest in peace."

"Ah, but does she, I wonder?"

"Well, I hope so. Seems like she never had much happiness on earth."

"She had a gift for doing the wrong thing."

Again Sarah paused in her work. "She tried, Althea. She meant well."

"Did she?" My hands dug down into the pockets of my white robe. "Did she really mean well? Did she ever stop to *think* whether she meant well? Why do we say that of people who always manage to do wrong?"

Sarah glanced at me apprehensively. "Now thy-ah, Althea—"

"Even aside from what she did to her own family," I plunged on, "she couldn't keep a friend. In some foolish way she always ended up exasperating people, baffling them. She didn't know truth from falsehood, or cruelty from self-righteousness. She was a genius for being mistaken, and she developed that injured-innocence complex. Why did she never *learn* anything?"

Sarah was watching me, aghast, and this goaded me the more. "Do you think she meant well by Kitty? Do you remember that summer when Kitty had to wear gloves because she bit her nails? How old was she—seven or eight? Someone laughed, at the start of it, at the little girl coming up from a swim with her sopping wet gloves buttoned on, and protested, 'But, Mildred, you *can't* keep this up!' Maybe that did it. Mother smiled a dim little smile and said, 'I can and I will.' All summer, all day, all night! It was unbelievable. Can you really say she meant well then?" I remembered some of Zebstrow's words. "It was obsessive, it was persecution. She couldn't leave the girl alone, she destroyed her friendships, poisoned her pets—she even saw to it that there was no intimacy between Kitty and me!"

Sarah was speechless, and I stopped, ran my hands through my hair, and massaged my temples. "It was weird," I finished. I was talking as much to myself as to Sarah. "All of her actions had a fatal weirdness, and the worst of it was that if you had to live with it you got used to it. You might say living with her was enough to drive anyone crazy."

Gently Sarah murmured, "It's all over and done with, Althea."

"Yes." A frustrated sigh came from me. "Yes. I suppose so. I hope so." I wrapped my robe closer.

"Go out and have your swim and forget it, now thy-ah."

In silence, without looking at her, I rested my fingers on her wrist; in silence she forgave me. I left her.

But a moment later, as I crossed the hall, a seemingly irrelevant question came out of the place in my mind where it had been lurking: was Kitty's bedroom door already open, after the shot, when I came to the door of my sitting room? Was she already there, or did we come to our doors simultaneously? My memory of the event had become a vacuum and I had never tried to recall any of the details. Even Zebstrow couldn't make me break into that sealed chamber.

I stood perfectly still in the dark hall. What was I asking myself? Was I asking if she, Kitty, might have had time to return to Mother's bedroom after the quarrel, take the pearl-handled revolver out of the bedside table, go into the dressing room and . . . (my eyes, my mind, refused to supply this part of the picture) . . . and get back to her own room without my having seen her as I approached my door?

Vertigo flooded me, my footsteps faltered, nausea rose in my throat.

Perhaps I should ask Rob, after all, for something, some tranquilizer, some antidote for the imagination.

A moment later I found myself running down over the lawn, running, running, all the way to the water.

What could go wrong, I asked myself that evening, in the grace of Father Bonneau's presence? The very thought calmed me, and, smiling, I dressed in a simple gown of yellow silk—not one of Branzini's inventions, but cut in a modest arc away from the throat—and I put on some topazes handed down in Mother's family. I was deeply tanned by now, and perhaps the lake water had freshened my eyes. It was true, I thought, looking at my reflection: my appearance had improved. Or should I say, altered. The alabaster vapidity of the earlier years was long gone, but after Branzini a confusion of the face took place and I couldn't tell what I looked like, although I used to catch glimpses in the mirror of the good bone structure (Daddy's, I hoped), and enormous eyes with dilated pupils.

Now everything of that desperation seemed erased, and the eyes were welcoming, or seeking welcome, the lips curved gently; the face of the reborn? I turned quickly away from the reflection. It frightened me. It was the face of a stranger. Its calm beauty accused me.

Kitty and Jack and the Goodfellows arrived together, striding down the length of the veranda with broad smiles, and something told me the girls had consulted each other in advance about their floor-length dresses, and altogether that they considered this a very special occasion and wanted me to know they did, and my words of greeting caught in my throat. I could only embrace them, including the Goodfellows with whom until then I'd only shaken hands, and drawing back they looked wonderingly into my face as Sarah had done that morning and as I had done, too, at my dressing table, and then they all began to talk at once, laughing, and at last I was able to ask Simon to make the drinks.

We sat in the screened-in portion of the veranda, and Kitty looked up automatically at the wind chimes, silent in the quieting of light and air. She felt my eyes on her and turned to smile at me, a smile of reassurance, I thought, or mutual congratulation, as if to say, We've come a long way, haven't we? She seemed to want to tell me she had put away dread and guilt for me, for tonight. She looked crisply fetching in white pique with a black velvet sash, and I guessed she had made the dress herself especially for tonight, not so much from the way she wore it, her spine straight, emphasizing its neat waist and bosom and full skirt, as from the way Jack looked at her in it, as if it gave her some extra measure of feminine potency and she were new to him.

Margo, in a flowing gown wildly splashed with oranges and purples and greens, her ears glittering with diamonds, made her little promotional burbles, encouraging laughter and lightly prodding us into a mood of festivity, and Simon, passing drinks, huffed and hissed through his teeth like some Oriental dignitary engaged in the ceremony of unbending. Bernice appeared, immensely consecrated, to offer canapés, and disappeared again.

Then Father Bonneau was seen approaching along the veranda, and a kind of Protestant hush fell as if at some awkward mistake. I rose, saying, "This is a very dear friend whom I've asked to join us," and he came up, smiling, weightless, his glance moving about but not actually alighting as I introduced him, and I saw the force of his simplicity communicating itself to the others, with its concomitant impression of ultimate worldliness, and their embarrassment changing to pleasure.

No one had met him before except Jack, who must be at least on speaking terms with everyone in the county, and for a second or two after the introductions no one knew quite how to proceed, but Father Bonneau murmured in his soothing accent, "What charming company for a summer evening," and sat down with us with a contented sigh. We reacted as if he had uttered an incantation. We *were* charming company, weren't we, and how lovely, how evanescent, he made the words "a summer evening"! He cast a spell; here, we felt, was a being artless and unspoiled enough to possess magic, the clue to life.

Jack's eye caught mine with a little twinkle; it took nerve or a sense of humor, he evidently believed, to include a priest in a Stillbrook in-group gathering. *They* had set out to make it a special occasion for me, but I was making it a very unusual one for them.

Would Father Bonneau have a drink, could he share with us in such a mundane ritual? "Yes," he replied to Simon's courtly inquiry. "If you have a little vermouth, and ice. . . ."

"A *cassis?*" whistled Simon, bowing in recognition of a fellow-sophisticate.

"A *cassis*, thank you," Father Bonneau responded obliviously, and turning to us he said, "You were all laughing when I arrived. I could hear it from the driveway and I stood still and listened, it sounded so beautiful, and I was afraid it would stop when I appeared."

Margo commenced one of her deep-chested, consoling chuckles. "It isn't hard for us to laugh at nothing, Father."

"Just because you are together?"

"Why yes, that must be it: because we're together."

"You are all old friends?"

"I am their new friend," I told him. Even my sister's new friend.

"That is what I could hear," he said, nodding. "The old friends laughing with a new friend."

"Are you a mystic, Father?" asked Kitty softly, grave and large-eyed, and the others waited with equal gravity for his answer. Right away, I thought, he had us speaking his language, an abstract language transcending boundaries of time and place, and it looked as if there would be no small talk tonight.

"Oh, I shouldn't be," he told Kitty gently. "I am supposed to be a realist. My church leaves very little to speculation."

Kitty pales rather than blushes. She did this now, and apologized, "Perhaps I shouldn't have—"

"No, no, it was a pleasing question," he assured her. "A very intuitive one. For you are right. Much of my feelings, perhaps my thinking, too, could be called mysticism, although I am a little bit alarmed by the word. It is vain of me, no doubt, but I like to think of it as a perception of truth."

"Yes," Kitty exclaimed, taking flight again in his unbounded space, "anyone who loves—" But again she recanted, her lip between her teeth, and glanced uncertainly at Jack. She wasn't used to voicing such thoughts in company, or to conversing with priests; was it ungraceful of her to reveal how much she was in her own element? Go ahead if you want to, Jack's quizzical eyes told her, and he almost looked as if he knew—for he was the one who understood her without words—what she wanted to say.

But Simon, loath to let the discussion die, interposed. "Must be both realist and mystic?" he suggested. He had got out a pipe and he leaned forward with his elbows on his knees, very much the old hand at abstract theorizing.

"I think what Mrs. Gilman was going to say," Father Bonneau amended diffidently, "was that anyone who loves perceives truth, a truth not mystical or real, but absolute and infinite."

There was an instant's silence.

Yes. I had it again, the answer, the shining all-inclusive answer. And again it was gone. Did Father Bonneau and Kitty have it all the time? And yet in my very ignorance, and because I had tasted more deeply of gall and wormwood, my momentary vision might come closer to the truth than theirs did, all the time.

What conceit! They were talking of love, I reminded myself, and what after all did I know of love? Murph? Branzini? My sister? Kitty and Father Bonneau lived in the territory of love. It was home to them, and I had only arrived at the threshold.

Kitty broke the silence, whispering, in awe, "Was I?" and everyone laughed indulgently.

How incongruous, this talk of love and mysticism on Mother's veranda! How at sea she would have been, how aghast! In the first place, she could only whisper the initials R. C., for Roman Catholic, behind her hand, so deplorable she considered it to be one. Imagine her consternation at finding a priest, a humble priest at that, relaxed in one of her rattan chairs! And there, even though seated on opposite sides of the circle, were Kitty and Jack, Katherine and Jack, united, beyond separation, a little larger than life in their oneness. And what would Mother have made of the far-out Margo and Simon? The whole impossible gathering might for once have made her doubt her sanity.

We dined in the glassed-in breakfast porch. With flowers and candlelight and Mother's best pink damask, the diamond-paned windows opened to the warm night, it was more intimate and more attractive than the baronial dining hall. Helga and Bernice had expended themselves to produce an elegant meal with accompanying wines, yet not too pretentious, and the gourmets were in seventh heaven. Simon, cued now and then by Jack, got started on Stillbrook folklore, hilarious legends that he recounted with an old-timer's accent, and I listened to the laughter as Father Bonneau had done, from a distance, rapturously.

It was a long time since I had heard shouts of laughter in Northwater, and I felt myself floating back to a happy dream. I was a child again, tucked up in bed upstairs, smiling to myself in the summer twilight as I listened to the sounds of conviviality below. First the rattle of Daddy's silver cocktail shaker, and then as the company arrived, the voices taking turns in different keys, words indistinguishable—a soprano here, a baritone there, and chorusing all together in an outburst of merriment, subsiding again to another solo; and lastly, as the cantata ended and the company moved indoors, a round unmodulated rumble from the dining hall, and then I drifted off to sleep. . . .

It was a sporting faction of the summer crowd that Daddy collected around him—handsome daredevil girls in white pleated skirts, scarves banded about their hair, and tanned, quick-moving men with sharply creased white trousers—all of them accomplished like Daddy at tennis, golf, dancing, "rather fast" according to Mother, more "common" than her own friends, who were actually inherited from her mama and papa, elderly folk who went hiking, or boating, or motoring, the very words spelling summer wholesomeness. . . .

In the middle of the night I might wake to the sound of the organ, groaning discordantly at the touch of inexpert revelers, or a roller-skating rattle as someone danced with the stuffed bear, and once I came down in the morning to find the Chinese war helmets rakishly perched atop the lowering heads of moose and water buffalo. (How had they got there? "Miss Sally duBose," Mother told me grimly. "The *gentlemen* hoisted her up. And," she added between her teeth, unable to restrain her fury, "she was *not* wearing bloomers.") The time came when Mother refused to go down to Daddy's parties and had supper with me in my sitting room, and then the parties ceased, and finally Daddy himself was gone. . . .

The silver cocktail shaker was shut up in its velvet-lined case, with its matching cups, and the organ was silent except for some rather eerie recitals, benefiting some worthy cause, and the bear went almost unnoticed in a dark corner by the entrance, and only the screams and giggles of loons disturbed the night. . . . But often in later summers I dreamed this dream, waking in the dark, thinking I heard the sound of laughter once more, coming from the veranda.

We were finishing dessert and Father Bonneau was talking about the remote peoples of the Andes, where he had been a missionary. The listening candlelit faces, suspended against the shadowed background, were like whimsical portraits of their owners by an impudent painter. Margo, her heavy lids downcast, her features wonderfully illuminated from below, was drawn as some Oriental divinity, floating serenely and unhelpfully in Lotus Land. Jack was himself at nine or ten, a serious, wiry, bright-eyed lad, his mother's son, his sister's brother, a faun-like youth with the assignment of responsibility already removing him from childhood. Kate, her heart-shaped face slightly tilted above her delicate neck, was a virginal girl-queen, destined to play a hapless role in history, and Simon, pale and elongated beside her, was the Cardinal who would plot her removal to the Tower. Father Bonneau was the hardest to caricature; no matter how one cast him, he would be himself. A scholar, perhaps, from a Russian novel, impractical, impoverished, lighthearted? No; the element of practicality, of strength, was too obvious, and there was something more elusive in his face than mere intelligence. . . .

Outside the open windows the crickets made their half-toned notes as if the night breathed, and the flowers within gave up a tropical fragrance. I knew suddenly I would never forget this moment, like the picture of the family around the pink watermelon, and even though I didn't have a limitless future in which to remember it, it was precious to me, and beautiful, and I memorized it with my senses, listening to it, holding its presence in my eyes.

The quiet voice broke off, the silver tooth flashed. "They were my children," said Father Bonneau, "and I go on too long about them." A little spell-breaking sigh rose around the table and the portraits stirred and became, again, my new friends.

We returned to the veranda, and after coffee Margo and Simon expressed a wish to see more of the house, and Kate volunteered to show them; she gave me her reassuring smile. She may have been granting me a few moments alone with Father Bonneau. Her hand touched Jack's arm. "Come with me," she said simply. "You've never really seen it either."

They went off, Margo's soaring exclamations leading them like an unfurling banner, and their voices faded into the interior of the house. The night sounds, from garden and lake, took over, and Father Bonneau and I sat for a time in silence, listening.

"You are more at peace?" he said at last. It was half-question, half-statement.

"Am I?" I asked, as if he were reading to me from a chart, as if peace, too, were as objective and foreign to my body as disease. I was in fact too much at peace at this moment to take myself seriously.

"It shows in your face."

"Is that what it is?"

"At least, the anger is gone."

"Anger, Father?"

"Well, something that refused, absolutely refused. Bitterness, perhaps? It was not a comfortable expression to look at. But there is still, in the eyes, something troubled."

"The burden of mortal sin, no doubt."

"It could not be much less. You say it lightly, but the eyes show you do not carry it lightly."

"No."

His voice was gentle, a little removed, not at all accusatory, but I suddenly realized that he, at least, was serious. I awoke then from my reveries. I saw myself as in a nightmare, crying out over the rose garden. A tightness painfully gripped my throat. "What must I do, Father? Must I make a confession?"

"I cannot tell you you must do that."

"Every time I see you, you lead me a step farther—I don't know where, or how, but you make the next step possible."

"We all seek for the same thing: for peace, for love."

"Peace and love are the same thing?"

"Oh yes, they have to be. How can there be peace without love?"

"You mean love of God, of course."

"I do, yes. You, perhaps, would mean love of life. Although, again, I do not think there is so much difference."

"There are people I love, too. I've discovered that."

"Yes, I could see it tonight. People are life as well."

I was smiling. "People and life and love and peace and God are all the same thing?"

"Certainly." He smiled, too. "I could not have put it better."

"And what about passion?" I asked, thinking about my recent torment. "Bodily passion? Where does that fit in?"

"Did you invent it?"

I had to laugh. "This is like a kindergarten catechism. No, Father; God invented it."

"As long as it is not your enemy, as long as you have a right to it, it too is good."

"Ah, goodness. Now we're talking about something else."

"Are we?"

The word "goodness" made me as uneasy as the word "joy." "Perhaps I've always thought of goodness as my enemy."

"Then it was not goodness."

There is no straying from the path, with him. The answer, the unseeable, the unreadable answer, always glimmers at the end of it. For him there are no pitfalls, no stumbling blocks, no sidetracks; his simplicity is his certainty.

"Tell me," he asked, "about this house."

Telling him about Northwater, even briefly, I realized, was like telling him the story of my life. But my voice was matter-of-fact; no fury rose to tremble in it. Father Bonneau listened in the shadows with the tips of his fingers pressed together and raised in an arch under his chin, the unconscious pose of the traditional listener, and when I finished he remained silent.

"You wonder," I asked at last, "why I chose to come back to such an unlucky place?"

He roused himself. "Oh no," he answered softly, "I do not wonder that." He made no further comment. He rose to his feet. "It grows late. Will you say good night for me to your guests?" The security of his presence at once began to drain from the evening. "I have enjoyed myself so much. Thank you." Desolately I took his hand. But what he said next shook me more than his departure, or any unspoken judgment. "I will pray for you."

I didn't anticipate that. I may have needed his prayers more than anything in life, but they terrified me.

There was still the last of the path to travel, the steepest, darkest, the most forbidding lap. *No!* I wanted to hold back. I wanted to implore him not to, not to pray for me; not yet!

But even as I was torn between need and reluctance, my empty hands clasping my throat, he was gone, and the impervious night noises closed over the departing sound of his car.

I stood alone on the veranda, cast back upon myself, my tedious self, upon Northwater. I had begun to feel feverish again. How, after all, could Father Bonneau's prayers alter anything?

Then with relief I heard faint voices within the house, and Margo's warble, and unable to endure my isolation another moment, I turned and hurried inside to them.

They were just coming down the stairs, slowly, musingly, chatting among themselves—Jack and Margo and Simon. I met them at the foot of the staircase. They read the question in my eyes and glanced about and behind them. "Where's Kitty?" they said, as though repeating my own words. "She was with us a second ago."

"Maybe she stopped off in one of those Pompeian bathrooms," Margo said, and sighed, gazing about her at the bristling walls. "Were they whimsical, the people who built these houses, or merely paranoid?"

" 'Tell me where is fancy bred,' " quoth Simon, " 'or in the heart or in the head?' "

But Jack, perturbed, was frowning at me. Neither of us liked Kitty's being upstairs alone. "I'll just go find her," I said, and left them.

The dim yellow wall lights in the upstairs hall serve merely to cloud the eyes. "Kitty?" I called softly. I stood still, listening. "Kitty?"

I must have known where she had gone. I must have believed she wouldn't play tricks on me, that malevolence wasn't in her nature, to lie in wait for me in the dark; I still believe it. It was one of those accidents of timing, and Kitty, thinking I was still with Father Bonneau, or not thinking at all but impelled by inner grieving, had simply taken advantage of the moment to linger behind and offer up her penance, perhaps even her prayer.

I turned the corner and went silently to Mother's room. Inside, the thick darkness was only faintly yellowed by the hall lights. I crossed the carpet toward the dressing room.

I stopped moving as if I had stepped off a precipice. *Mother!* She was bent over the dressing table once more, in her long white dress, her forehead resting on the glass. . . .

A scream (whose? mine?) rose and split the darkness, seemed to pierce all the rooms of the house. A familiar pain stabbed me, I was falling steeply, groping in the black rushing air, and even after the white figure moved and became Kitty I continued to fall, pain and darkness engulfing me until the last pinpoint that was myself disappeared in space . . . and, like a tiny light, went out. . . .

I no longer have the will, one might almost say the inclination, to fight this disease, this inexorable adversary, as if I could win. There is no more glory in hand-to-hand combat. Even as a mental breakdown patient, in Zurich, I submitted to the techniques of therapy ill-humoredly, often hurling oaths, sweet and obnoxious by turns. (And how deaf, how silent, they had become, the sanitarium personnel, in their patience!)

But in the Stillbrook hospital, these past two weeks, I looked for the first time for tenderness, and tenderness came from hands and voices, and there was something coolly refreshing in this surrender, some incomprehensible clue to Father Bonneau's *goodness*, in giving myself up to the ministrations of others. The expression on Rob's face, however grave, was one of satisfaction; unconditionally, I was letting him help me.

Again I shake my head at myself, belatedly learning

the fundamental lessons of life. This business of giving and receiving: is it reversible? Is it very complicated, or very simple?

Certainly I have come out of the hospital in better shape than I came out of the session before, when I fought it out alone, at Northwater. But without a will. Without the innate desire to survive, at any cost.

Perhaps this is the necessary softening-up, before I take the next terrifying step along the path Father Bonneau has opened to me. Once, in the first day or two at the hospital, Kitty's stricken face hovered in a haze of fever and narcosis, and I wondered if this were indeed the end. But I knew it wasn't; even in delirium I knew there was still to be a reckoning and I wouldn't be let off that easily.

With an immense effort I groped through the haze to find my voice. My lips were swollen and unmanageable. "Kitty, wait. Until I'm better. Don't come. Can't bear . . . see me like this. Torture yourself. Please. Rob send for you." Something like that. She stayed away. It was cruel of me perhaps; perhaps not. I trusted Jack to comfort her.

He appeared some days later. He told me at once, "I came on my own. Kitty didn't send me." Was he angry? His little smile was missing. "Can I sit down a minute? Do you feel up to it?"

"Yes. I'm much better. I'm going home soon."

"So Rob told me." He took the chair facing me, folded his arms and crossed his ankles neatly. He said, "There are no more secrets, Althea. I've had a talk with Rob and he gave it to me straight."

"Yes. That's all right."

"And I gave it straight to Kate, too."

I turned my face away. "Yes. I suppose that had to be done. There's no more point in trying to hide anything."

"No. In a way, I admire your guts." He corrected himself. He didn't believe in using crudities with a woman. "Courage."

"Guts is all right," I told him.

"In another way, I don't." The absence of humor in his eyes alarmed me, all the more so because I could still see behind them the responsible boy of nine or ten. "Did you think you were doing us a favor, your own sister and brother-in-law?"

"I didn't want it—this sickness—to influence her! I explained it to Rob, it would louse everything up!"

"Goddammit, excuse me, are you saying you didn't think Kate could take it?"

"Jack, she's taken so much—"

"She has!" He got to his feet and stood staring out the window, his fists rammed in his pockets. There was a kind of morality in the purity of his temper and his effort to control it, and it silenced me. He turned at last and sat down again. "She has. Althea, when we got married I knew what her life had been like. I knew everybody else her age had a headstart on her, and on top of everything she had just been through her mother's suicide. But I made up my mind I wasn't going to baby her, be a big brother to her, or a father, so as to shield her from everything. She had a *husband*, and I thought it would be better for her to feel I had a wife. What I'm trying to say, I wanted to give her the chance to catch up. I didn't want her to be afraid to be herself."

Now at last he laughed, a short gasp or two. "Me and my big ideas! Maybe I thought I was getting a child-bride or something. I can tell you, I had some surprises coming to me." A beam of remembered delight shone in his eyes. "She didn't need to catch up, she needed a chance to start right in. She was more woman than I had any idea of, in lots of ways she was more grown up than I was." Quizzically he tilted his head and pulled an ear lobe. "Althea, *something* was going on in that girl all the while, growing up. She always *was* herself. She had to learn how to take it, and she did learn, but it didn't make a weakling out of her. Yes, she's quiet, and small, gentle, but she's got a backbone of steel."

"I know this, Jack. I knew it."

"Then why," the anger again, "why, may I ask, have you been trying to protect her from something she has a right to know?"

"I tried to tell you: I wanted to get to know her without this abominable illness hanging over our heads. I didn't want her to pity me! I wanted us to be ourselves."

"How could you be yourselves when you were practicing a deception?"

How indeed? It might have been Zebstrow talking.

"She's not a poor little mistreated child any more, Althea, and she's not alone. There's two of us, husband and wife. We knew there was something wrong ever since you got back, and being your nearest relatives, your only relatives, we had a right to share it with you." He was thoughtful an instant, and shook his head. "No, it's more Kate I'm concerned about, it's your lack of respect for her—"

"Jack, lack of respect!"

"That's what it amounts to, isn't it? I told you once, Kate needs you. I think it might finish off all those leftover feelings from Northwater if you respect her as she is now." He shook his head again. "Oh hell, I'm getting out of my depth, and I didn't come here to upset you. That's the last thing I wanted to do." His eyes suddenly leveled on mine with a piercing intensity. "Althea, all I came for was this: I came to ask you to stop trying to put us off, and to let us help you in whatever way we can."

Silenced again, I put out my hand and he reached forward at once to take it. I had an almost unbearably clear look just then into Kate's world with Jack. There was such a lovely sentimental coziness about it, even aside from its setting of the old house and the double bed and the gleaming little kitchen.

And how sweet was Jack's brotherliness to me, his strong calloused hand! For a moment I could let myself feel like one of his own family. There was a great soothing corniness about him to which I abandoned myself, a greeting-card corniness, a Mother's Day corniness. No one would go hungry or lonely if he could help it; he stood by, ready to lend a hand, shoulder a burden, right a wrong.

It was the kind of security Mother must have known he would give Kate, a lower-middle-class security, a fellowman responsibility that Mother disdained, that for some reason frightened her. She had been raised to perform kind deeds herself, in the role of Lady Bountiful, with cool white hands, pretty baskets, generous donations, not to be publicized. Why then did she abhor Jack's family conscience, as if it were just slightly obscene? Because it involved intimacy? Because it involved love—personal, robust, elemental love?

I thanked him. "There'll be no more deception, Jack. I do respect Kate. I've always respected her." A shaking laugh broke from me. "But I had big ideas, too. It must be that she brings out the champion in us. I wasn't going to let anything stand in the way of your marrying her."

He grinned, rising. "I wasn't either."

And after he had gone one or two weak tears, of gratitude, of relief, trickled into my temples.

Father Bonneau appeared every day, on his hospital rounds. I would open my eyes and he would be there, just inside my door, or at my bedside. In the beginning, when I was in pain and only half-conscious, he touched my wrist, we smiled at each other like conspirators, and no words were spoken. But his being in the room was a kind of grace. And always after he left something was clarified, something—distilled and already determined—effaced the spurious hospital odor of sanctity, rendered the humiliating affixtures of tubes and ice packs merely sensible; soothed the racked flesh itself. Later, after I began to rally, he would say softly, almost absent-mindedly, like a person humming to himself, "You are better today?" And I would answer yes, and he would nod, lift his hand—half in salute, half in blessing—and drift away.

The morning I left the hospital I asked him, "Have you been praying for me?"

"Oh yes," he told me, mildly and unequivocally, but again as if his mind were elsewhere, or everywhere.

I studied him for a moment. "I was afraid of your prayers. I was procrastinating; I thought I had plenty of time."

"And now you are not afraid?"

"Now I had better have them."

"Yes," he agreed. He moved to the door, and turned. "If you believe in my prayers, why not try one of your own?" I must have looked aghast; he smiled, his spectacles making wayward lights. "It would do no harm. God likes prayers from those who try it even when they aren't sure of Him."

I was stubborn and awkward again. How could he say so readily and affectionately what God liked? "Why?" I asked him.

His brow furrowed, as if he felt he must delve into the fundamentals of faith for me. But he smiled once more, dismissing the task, and glancing at me contritely, he summed it up, "Because He knows it isn't easy."

And now I am back at Northwater as good as new, better than new, or so I like to think. When you've been away and you come back and look into your old mirror, for a second or two you can see whatever changes have taken place. I saw today that the seeking look was gone, replaced with something found.

I called Kitty as soon as I got home and asked her to come and see me. She looked so forbidding, entering my sitting room, her black brows scowling, that I knew she was fighting down an explosion of tears. She seated herself in the wicker chair, and I said, "Go ahead and cry, Kitty," and she cried at once, wholeheartedly, but with scarcely a sound, dropping her face into her hands and bending over her knees. She turned away, wiping her cheeks with the back of her fists, whispering with tears again, and wiping, and I passed her the Kleenex without saying anything. She blew her nose, and at last she turned to me again, wet-eyed, and grimaced a smile.

"I haven't cried at *all* until now," she told me thickly, "and I *wasn't* going to."

"I'm glad you did then, you needed to." I hadn't expected her to cry, not after Jack's dissertation, and I found I admired her tears more than her stoicism. It seemed braver of her to cry openly. But I was unmoved by her tears, because it was me she wept for, the sister she was to lose; she was crying for someone I couldn't feel sorry for.

Her wide gaze now seemed to surround me. She said, wonderingly, "I've always been intimidated by you. You've always been so—remote, so unapproachable. I'm not intimidated now. And it's not your sickness that's done it, but," she looked amazed, "my tears."

"Yes." This, too, was in some way part of the giving and receiving lesson. "I'm glad."

"Althea, that night, of your dinner party, when you found me in Mother's dressing room—"

"Forget it, Kitty."

"No, I feel terrible about it. I had no idea you would—"

"I know, I know. Forget it. I was already sick."

Her eyes roved away from me. "I couldn't help myself, going in there. We had made such light of the house, Margo and Simon and I, laughing at its weird pretentiousness, and suddenly I had to—apologize to *her*." She halted abruptly.

I studied Kitty. Does Jack really know this girl? She is like one of those dark Scottish lakes, beautiful and bewitching, and bottomless; not hard to fathom but unfathomable, a mystery, as she said, even to herself.

She got to her feet. "Althea, may I come to see you every day, or nearly every day, just for a minute or two?"

A week ago I would have shrunk from this suggestion, the demands of such intensified sisterhood. Now, I answered, "Yes. Please do."

I meant it. I had never learned stoicism, and her tears had washed more of my old defenses away, and I remembered that terror still hovered in the offing, loomed even closer, and I realized that her appearance every day might anchor me to reality, warding off phantoms, and that I needed someone to make of me the demands of kinship.

"And, Althea," she went on earnestly, "if you should want to come to us—I mean, this *is* such a haunted house, I don't like to think of you alone here. As a matter of fact it was Jack's idea. We'd like to have you with us."

"God, no!" It sounded like the old me. I laughed; I hadn't changed all that much. "Thank you, love, but I guess I'm still a creature of solitude. I'm supposed to take it easy for a few days, and then I'll be up and around as usual. Bernice looks after me. Rob drops in every day, too. I want to be here. I have to be here."

"Yes," she consented, but she stood looking down at me with a sad bafflement. "I can't help feeling," she said softly, "that you're waiting for something here. Hoping, maybe, to solve something."

"Maybe I am."

"Concerning Mother?"

My brow wrinkled: what did I need to solve concerning Mother? Her eyes, softly glowing, watched me. I said, "I suppose you could put it that way."

"Don't," she advised me in a whisper. She smiled. "You asked me not to torture myself. You mustn't do it either."

I shivered, sucking in my breath. We were staring at each other with almost the same prolonged, horrified fascination that had held us on opposite sides of the hall, eleven years ago.

I said, "I'll try not to." Anything to break that hypnotic deadlock.

I lifted my arms to her, and she bent and briefly rested her cool cheek against mine.

In August we usually have a foretaste of fall. The wind lifts and the humidity drops, and the day dawns cold and sparkling. Yesterday Bernice lit the fire in my sitting room.

Rob examined the book I had been trying fitfully to read and returned it to the foot of my chaise, and settled back in the wicker chair and studied me.

"Is something bothering you?" he asked quietly. "I get the feeling of some tension in you, something on your mind. Is there anything I can do?"

"You do enough. You're a busy man. Your coming to see me is more than I could ask for."

He didn't want my gratitude; his bleached eyebrows twisted unreceptively. We have achieved a kind of inactive intimacy in which we can sit in silence for long minutes, gazing at each other and thinking our own thoughts. The wind sighed, tossing the boughs of the great pines beyond my window, a stressful time-hurrying sound, but here the fire popped and hissed softly, and the room was snug with the scent of wood smoke. He said at last, "I find you restful."

I was amused. "Nobody ever said that to me before."

"I mean, I *am* busy, always in summer, and it's restful to sit here quietly for a little while, with you."

With you. He added it with the faintest reluctance, but honestly. Honesty compels me to add; but make nothing of it. Ah, Rob, it is indeed restful! Because after you leave, the torment, the fire of body-longing smoulders again, darts up in inopportune flames, and I ask myself, Why can't you be as honest? Why not reach out to him, put your arms around him, seduce him if need be, implore him—?

It must be that I love this man, and the sense of mercy holds me, in his presence, leaving him to himself.

I asked, "How can I be tense and restful at the same time?"

"It's I who rests."

"No, I do, too, while you're here. I've never felt so safe. Don't smile, it's a nice way to feel. Of course I have things on my mind. There isn't much time left, and I must somehow make restitution for a misspent life."

"Don't be flippant with me, Althea."

"It's an old habit, darling. Forgive me."

"It's odd: I don't care anything about your misspent life, I don't care to know about it, but I'm a little—well, resentful of it. I would like to think of you as always being as you are now."

"Which is what?"

"Vulnerable. That's the first word that comes to mind; I'm not skillful with words as you are. But, vulnerable, compassionate—"

"*Good?*"

"You're being flippant again. Certainly good. Althea, in this restitution of yours, don't give yourself too hard a time."

I regarded him feeling older and wiser and unspeakably less worthy. I was jealous of the person he thought I was. A knife turned in me. I said, "Have you ever looked up your father's records of me?"

"No. Why should I?" His honest blue eyes filled with misgiving, saying, Don't tell me, don't tell me anything I don't need to know.

"He patched me up," I told him doggedly, "after a couple of third-rate abortions. The first one when I was fourteen, and again when I was fifteen or sixteen."

Rob turned to look out the window. His face, freckled and sunburnt, had drained underneath of color.

"That's just a sample," I told him.

"Althea," he breathed in protest, his eyes still turned to the tossing pine boughs.

I leaned my cheek against the cushion behind me and shut my eyes. Why had I done this, deliberately appalling him? For his own good, or for mine—because his tender respect appalled me? Some gritty self-respect of my own seemed to have prompted me; it was all very well that he cared nothing about my misspent life, but if he were to accept me as I am he must accept me as I was.

He will sigh now, I thought, and leave, and when he next stops to see me he will be stern and on his guard again.

I opened my eyes. He was regarding me with an expression I couldn't read; there was some humor in his eyes and some sorrow, an indistinguishable mixture. He said, "You didn't have to tell me this."

I held my breath.

He smiled. "Once I might have been—disappointed, disapproving, even. But you forget: I've learned something about mercy." He got up, pressed my crossed ankles in farewell, and added, "From you. See you tomorrow." And went away.

I ask myself, Was I given love to add to my suffering or to add to my joy? Was I given it so that I might know it, once?

And then, another hallucination. She appeared again, last night. She was standing in the door between my bedroom and the sitting room—dressed in white as usual, wearing the broad-brimmed straw hat, and carrying over her arm a basket of white roses. She stood there smiling a sly little smile, her moist dark eyes fastened on mine, compelling me. She didn't speak. Slowly she raised her hand, crooked a finger revoltingly, and slowly beckoned. . . .

"No!" With a single convulsion of the body I flung myself back, away from her, and huddled, knees doubled up, against the headboard of my bed. She beckoned again with the one hideous finger. "*No!* Not yet!"

She must have gone away. When I awoke this morning I was still in an uncomfortable huddle among the pillows, my arms clasped about my knees. I stretched out, shivering, slid down under the blankets and moaned with relief and dread.

Something must be done. I can't think my way out of this. I can't die my way out. Rob can't reach it with potions. I'll sleep in the daytime, I told myself, and stay awake all night. I had to laugh.

Why, with an insistent feeling of innocence, and the end inevitable anyway, am I seeing these apparitions?

In a panic I got up and began to dress, but my shaking fingers fumbled and I rang for Bernice. "But it is too soon," she protested, fastening my collar, "the doctor said you were not to drive the car until he gave permission—!"

The church was empty again. I sat and watched the gleaming crucifix. I sensed around me the thousands of prayers that had been uttered here, hovering over me in the air, still softly churning amongst themselves like motes of dust in a shaft of light. I made myself get down on my knees. I bowed my head, shutting my eyes and emptying thought and feeling into my own darkness. God, I began, timidly addressing Father Bonneau's God, the God to whom all these prayers around me had been addressed, God—?

I didn't know what to ask for, or how to ask.

A side door was flung open and the black-haired rectory maid burst in with a watering can. She sped across the church to the altar, bobbed in a quick genuflection, and like a bee began to dart from vase to vase, replenishing the gladioli.

I rose and approached her. I spoke in French, to spare us another mangled debate. "Is Father Bonneau in the rectory?"

A powerful arm shot into the air, and she was one of

those wartime posters of La Belle France, mouth open in a call to arms, lacking only the little cap with the tricolor. He was in Quebec on vacation! Father Ryan was substituting! Father Bonneau would not be back until Saturday! She wheeled, bobbed her knee, charged past me breathing onions, crossed the church again, slammed the door.

Silence settled once more. I stood for a moment with a trespassing finger on the altar. The time for asking, for questions, was over. Now it was the silent church, the squirming prayers of past supplicants, and a great, moody, watchful God of my own invention, that seemed to question me.

They were making aprons in Margo's living room, a place I hadn't thought would lend itself to homely pastimes. For an instant, coming in from the bright outdoors, I saw the three women in the vaulted room in terms of painting again, the out-of-fashion *genre* kind in which every rustic detail is lovingly illumined against a somber background—the faces lifted and turned to me, the hands poised over the folds of flowered chintz, the scissors and scraps and a spool on the polished floor. Kitty, her features aglow in the island light of a sewing machine, smiled without speaking, as if there were no need to greet me since our line of communication had never been broken, and Ginny, with a barely audible, begrudging, "Hi," ducked her head again.

"We're making them for the hospital bazaar," Margo explained. "My God, I'll see these roses in my dreams. How my old analyst in New York would pounce; symbols of some disgusting infantile phase, no doubt. All right, girls, what do you say: end of Occupational Therapy. I invited Althea for coffee."

"You're the last person," said Ginny, determinedly sewing on, her voice straining against dammed-up antagonisms, "who I'd have thought would need an *analyst.*" She uttered the word with the would-be amusement, the thinly disguised abhorrence Mother would have used for the word "sex."

"Appearances are deceiving," Margo answered blithely, fishing about her feet for scissors and scraps. She added, straightening, "I console myself with the thought that people without neuroses are boring."

"Well, now," said Ginny, snapping a thread with her teeth, her voice suddenly enriched with warning, "I don't think *Rob* is neurotic." He was useful to her ego, I realized then, as an unimpeachable husband as well as a tiresome appendage, according to the turn of the conversation.

"Rob is sometimes boring," Margo replied, with an irrepressible chortle, and Kitty and I had to laugh, more at her than with her. (Rob, Rob, my shining knight, a private voice crooned in me: Yes, sometimes you are boring.) Ginny flushed darkly and opened her mouth to remonstrate. "Forgive me, love," Margo cut in, "I couldn't resist the opening. Rob is superb, as we all know. Put down the damned apron now and come help me. You're the only woman in the world who knows how to help in someone else's kitchen without getting in the way."

Promptly Ginny put away her sewing and rose to follow Margo, but only partly mollified; patches of red, like birthmarks, still mottled her cheeks and temples.

Kitty smiled at me again, commentless, unasking; she seemed absorbed, almost secretive, as though she harbored some inner, insulating preoccupation that served as a source of passivity toward outer beings.

And once more I had the feeling that Ginny was in a huff, perhaps without knowing it, at me rather than Margo, that peace had reigned before my appearance. I was touched by her automatic obedience, child-like, to Margo's summons; does she compensate for her hostilities with service? And I admired as something quite mature, quite sophisticated, the genial tolerance of her friends, the forgiveness that must stem from compassion. I can't believe she suspects me of seducing Rob, or Rob of being enamored of me; he is good, his ethics are sterling, and she knows this, but I can't believe she esteems him enough to think of him as desirable to another woman. She knows me hardly at all. We have never exchanged more than two or three words; she avoids speaking to me directly. It must be my *type* that gets under her skin: the vagabond being, the glittering and irresponsible, bejeweled and emaciated, who appears to have tasted all the known forbidden fruits and dwelt in all the exalted palaces and yet chooses to invade this simple, principled corner of the world. It could be that she envies as well as despises me.

Rob can't have told her the nature of my illness (ethics again, or lack of communication?), for I'm certain if she knew it she would feel more kindly toward me, a guilty dutiful kindness, and this certainty doesn't make me like her more.

Kitty was closing her sewing machine. "It's high treason, I suppose," she said, "but I've gone over to the handwork booth."

She was talking about the hospital bazaar. "Yes," I said, remembering. "You always used to work for Mother at the flower booth." I have one stray picture of her there, dim and dispirited in the canvas-hot recesses of Mother's tent, filling vases from a tub of water which doubled as a container for wounded, drowning water lilies.

God, the hospital bazaar! What a turmoil *that* created at Northwater. Everyone up at dawn to cut flowers, the station wagon loaded like a hearse, the voice coming clearly from the drive, "Katherine, you will go in and *put* on another dress, you *do* have a clean one I trust, I will *not* have you at my booth looking like an *in*mate of an *asylum*. And *try* to smile, just *try*, for *once*. And on your way, tell Sarah I *need* . . ." I buried my head under my pillows and wished I could stay there until it was all over.

Traditionally held the last week in August, the bazaar was the climax, socially and organizationally, of the summer, and the whole town and all the summer people united to put it over. For weeks ahead Mother sailed about with her glasses hung about her neck and her lists in hand, issuing orders, cajoling in a liquid voice over the telephone, creating all about her an obscure, sullen confusion. No one on her committee could make a move without her, no one knew what move she would next want made; meetings were peremptorily called, overflowing the veranda, and adjourned without resolving anything. She couldn't go about an executive task quietly and devotedly, or gaily; she gave it an immense importance, and inevitably her cohorts came to feel it wasn't all that important. Kitty wasn't the only one: all of Mother's committee labored for her with the same soulless resignation.

"And you," said Ginny, returning to the living room with a tray, and, I surmised, addressing me, "what booth did *you* work on?" Without looking at me she smiled, rather woodenly, to cover the sneer that had crept willy-nilly into her voice.

"I never went near the place if I could help it."

In spite of herself she stared at me now as if I had uttered heresy; she had of course expected an admission of nonparticipation, but this shocked her. The hospital bazaar was more sacred to Ginny Clay than it was to Mother. She clamped her lips shut as if she would never speak to me again and turned away, and her hair, even her clean straight brown hair, condemned me.

"Oh yes," I continued, the irrepressible laughter, like Margo's, commencing to rise within me too, and some familiar tone roused Kitty and she glanced at me apprehensively, "I have a phobia about concerted worthy efforts and the executive tendencies of women. They never fail to horrify me. All that organized, energetic good will! What self-infatuation! I am always aware of the inherent hostilities in exalted lady-administrators." Ginny refused to turn her head. Why must the girl *make* one dislike her so? Make me make her dislike me? Why couldn't I woo her better self as the others did with flattery and forbearance? "I become paralyzed," I went on heedlessly. "They render me more useless than I am, these capable women and their zingy campaigns—they make me undedicated, profane. They bring out the worst in me. I want to shout four-letter words, create havoc." I shrugged. "It's better not to have me around."

Ginny sat pale and frozen. (Would she report this to Rob? I hoped so.) Margo betrayed her presence on the threshold with a snort, and then broke into wholehearted laughter.

Soothingly Kitty interposed, "But you did go to the bazaar at night sometimes."

"Of course," I admitted. "When the chuck-a-luck games started, and the workers behind the booths were having surreptitious drinks, and a little wickedness freshened the air." Ginny's eyes were now shut tight. And I saw myself at the bazaar as if far away, small, disdainfully entering the milling crowd with my friends, incognito as it were in my court of admirers and hangers-on; so far away, so insignificant and misguided, that I seemed to envisage another person, my own orphan.

"And then someone usually gave a big party," Kitty added, the sentence ending flatly, for she had never gone to one herself, even though all the bazaar workers from all the booths were invited. ("We will come home sensibly to bed," Mother decreed, at supper. "You and I, Katherine, are not carousers. Leave the gay whirl to Althea." She reached over and patted my hand. And she went on dreamily, with her dim smile, "It's depressing enough to see you in the same room with Althea at a club dance, but in your present bedraggled condition it would be downright disgraceful." Kitty had already acquired, then, a habit of shifting her eyes and gazing off into space as if she hadn't heard a word. . . .)

And now, over coffee in Margo's living room, I found myself saying, "I shall give one myself this year and you shall come."

"A party?" A wide clown-grin, evidently used for good news, spread across Margo's face. "A real party?"

"A real party."

"In that marvelous house?"

"Of course. A party to end parties."

"Althea, do you think—" Kitty began anxiously.

"The works. Champagne. Music. Japanese lanterns."

"Japanese lanterns!" Margo wailed, transported.

"Certainly. They must be stored away somewhere. Daddy used them."

Ginny came out of her stony pose. "I don't think anyone could enjoy a thing like that," she said primly, "after all day at the bazaar. We'll be much too tired."

"Oh nonsense, Ginny, you know perfectly well we always celebrate somehow, even though nobody's given a real party lately. Last year we didn't get to bed 'til three."

"And anyway," Ginny continued, gathering up her sewing things to depart, "I'm talking as if I were invited."

Margo opened her mouth and, evidently not trusting herself, shut it.

"But you must come, Ginny," I said gently. "I am inviting you."

She shot me a glance curiously filled with something like terror, as if my voice had just for an instant penetrated her defenses and she saw plainly the gracelessness I evoked from her. "Well, thank you," she answered stiffly, another flush rising in her cheeks, and it was I who felt guilt, a sinking inner cry of pity. But she couldn't resist adding, "If I'm not too tired."

Margo rose with her, putting an arm about her shoulders. "Love, you're never tired."

"Oh yes I am, sometimes." She sounded thin and childlike again. She was close to tears. "Who wouldn't be, with seven children?"

Hurriedly she made her departure.

No one had the heart to speak of her, after she had gone. There was a tiny silence, and then Kitty and I rose simultaneously to go, too.

"We needed you in our midst," Margo said to me, at her door. She didn't enlarge on the statement; she gave me her wide grin. I thought about it, puzzled, going down the covered stairs to the parking area.

But the rushing stream on the other side of the house was audible again, and my steps slowed as the sound ruffled over me like a breeze, seeking out and reopening in me a little cache of stored happiness. My gaze lifted to the foliage surrounding us, some eye-clarifying solution seeming to surge up in my vision, and I was amazed that it was my right to possess so pure and delightful a memory, and I hoped that innocent Sunday was stored somewhere within Rob, as well.

"Althea, really, is it wise to do this party thing?"

We had paused between our cars on the shaded gravel, Kitty's hand on her door handle, the woods grave about us, their weight and eminence dissolved in the unending shout of the stream.

I was impatient with her moody voice, the blurred inner concern of her face. "It isn't, darling, but I'm exempted from wisdom now."

"Are you?" Sorrow stood in her heavy, level eyes.

I sighed. "You and Father Bonneau. Oh Kitty, let me have a last fling! No, it isn't just for me. Or for you. Or for Daddy. I'd like to do it for Northwater, so that everyone will remember it as gay and carefree."

"You think you can cancel all the unhappiness there in one evening, with a party?"

I turned away from her eyes. "Kitty, stop. What's eating you?"

"Murder," she said, for the second time.

She spoke the word very softly, but it fell like a crushing weight on the back of my neck, on my eyelids, on my brain.

Slowly and without sound I pounded the hood of the Ferrari. "Kitty, don't. Don't. Don't."

"The self-murder," she went on, "that took place in that house." And her new, passive smile made her voice all the more desolate. "All right, have your party. Let me help you. I just don't want to lose you any sooner than I have to."

"My God, you're in a chilling mood, aren't you?"

She opened her car door. "I don't know," she answered thoughtfully. "I feel very far from fantasizing or romanticizing or evasions. I'm in a sort of black-and-white mood."

"Well, I am not." I turned on her. "Call it fantasy or romanticism or evasion, but I have found a little happiness for the first time in my life and I'd like to hang on to it!"

She was seated in the station wagon now, the door still ajar. "Althea, Althea . . ." Tears spilled down her cheeks.

I moved to her quickly, took her hand, pressed it to my face. Jack was right; there are times when I feel she is the invalid and not I, that I must protect her, sustain her, save her. "Oh, Kitty, what's the matter with us? Is this the normal strain of a time like this? Forgive me!"

She smiled, brushed the tears from her cheeks with the back of her hand, and then delved in her bag for a handkerchief. "Forgive me, too. I don't know what's come over me. Good-by. I'll drop in tomorrow." And she drove off.

She is part of myself, I thought, watching the car disappear down the wooded drive. I don't know, either, what's come over her, what she is thinking or compounding, but her mysteries are my mysteries. I wait now for something, some signal, from her perhaps, and my waiting is patient, unexpectant, steadying. I will be what she makes of me; I must suffer if she suffers. I don't know if she has grown more and more strange, since my return, or more and more real; I must accept her strangeness as real.

And again I thought how savage the word was on her sensitive lips: *murder.*

The summer draws to a close in sulky heat. There is a slothful threat in the air, as though morning after morning a vast outspread dragon yawns, monstrously heaves and turns over, goes back to sleep again. Nothing happens. The dormant day is milk-white, heavy as lead; a crimson disc sets in a pewter haze, and at night heat-lightning flickers menacingly, like a forked tongue, over the horizon. "Need rain *awful* bad," Clarence complains, pronouncing awful as offal; but no rain comes. Little rainbows hover over the lawn while Clarence runs the sprinklers.

The machinery for the party has been set in motion. Bernice, more magisterial than before, heady with power, bit in teeth, has again assumed command. She passes judgment on my suggestions with pursed lips, offers counter-suggestions, attends to subpreparations that haven't occurred to me. The electric bulbs on antlers and wrought-iron chandeliers are replaced, rented floor-polishers whine, the piano is tuned. I call her *mon general*, which she accepts without amusement. Unlike Mother, she doesn't create confusion, however noisy her deployments; everything gets done with a cumulative precision, and soon the machinery is running more and more smoothly instead of less and less so, producing a cool, depersonalized atmosphere in the house in contrast to the heat of the day.

I flee to the dock. I escape from the intolerable buildup, which feels like the approach of doom. I almost wish, like Kitty, that I hadn't decided to give the party; I'm thankful that Bernice has taken it out of my hands. Lulled by the desultory slapping of water against wood, I make up for the long waking hours at night, the insomnia I've developed without trying.

Murph comes back to me in my dreams. I am running for my life away from him down the night-dark main street of Stillbrook. . . . I dance with Branzini under baroque chandeliers, and he whispers seductively in my ear, "You think you're terribly clever, don't you?"

I used to contend with Zebstrow that my dreams weren't wishful, that they revealed to me the truth I couldn't face awake. So I try to interpret these ambiguities, and instead doze off again.

I dream of Zebstrow, seeing him as I once saw him in Zurich, at an outdoor café. I was passing in a taxi on my way back to the sanitarium after a shopping trip, and I recognized him having coffee with his wife. She wore the neat dark suit European women wear so well and she was reading a newspaper, while he sat facing the sun with his eyes shut, his face sallow and lumpy like an old prize-fighter's. They looked like any contented bourgeois couple. I was embarrassed; I had never seen Zebstrow outside the sanitarium before, I had never seen his wife, and I had the feeling of having spied on his private life; I shouldn't even have noticed, I felt, his wife's stout walking shoes. I never told him about it afterward.

But in my dream his eyes open and fasten on mine.

From café to taxi, they pinion me like talons. I shrink back in my seat but they follow me, and then slowly he lifts an arm, clenches his fist, and gives me the Communist salute.

I wake up laughing. I turn over and stare at the white sky. I shudder; his eyes still follow me. And what is the symbolism of the salute: comrades under the skin? Workers of the world, unite? Freedom? Menace? I give up; I am not terribly clever, especially not awake.

Rob's visits are less frequent. He is swamped with the accumulation of summer and year-round patients. He drives in hurriedly, finds me on the wharf, takes my temperature, touches my wrist, squints into my eyes, asks a question or two, utters a word of advice, departs.

Once, waking there from a deep sleep, I found him crouched beside me, his unguarded face meditative, heavy with care, and I felt for the first time that I was younger and he older. We looked at each other without moving, unsmiling, as if we had met on a bridge over a chasm in the middle of nowhere. And then, as my longing commenced, he stirred, and I sat up with a sigh. We went into the routine of questions and answers, and he left.

In a rage—at myself, at him, at Fate—I plunged into the water.

Happiness, I said, too recklessly, to Kitty, claiming a little of it! Even then the word had an impermanent sound, and on paper, also, it takes wing. It doesn't seem to belong with the great abstracts, love and God and peace. I yearned to see Father Bonneau again.

And as if in answer, his voice on the telephone this morning. "I am back from my vacation. I have been praying for you. How are you feeling?"

The charming accent, the door opening wide once more on sanctuary, and I realized, overwhelmingly, how much I needed to know he was nearby. "Oh, Father," I began, suddenly all to pieces, as if I would shake apart. I couldn't go on. I licked tears that weren't there from my lips.

"I am going out to make some calls," he said. "If it would be convenient—"

"Oh yes, please come!"

We sat on the veranda. The house was quiet; perhaps my general, ever on the watch, ordered this, too. I clasped my hands and leaned forward hungrily as if to substantiate in Father Bonneau's material presence my immaterial belief in him. Had I only imagined his tranquil goodness? Was it really there for me to feast on, however vicariously?

He said, "Do not be discouraged."

My clasped hands flew to my mouth.

"Or afraid," he added.

I tried to calm myself. I said slowly, "I went to your church to pray, but no prayer would come. I don't think your God likes me."

He smiled. "He likes you better than you do."

"You know Him so well!" I cried, half-jeering.

"Yes," he agreed quietly. "But not as well as He knows me."

"Father, I can't *ask* Him for anything!"

"Oh yes; you can. And you do not have to go to my church to do it. You can ask Him for what He thinks you need. That is not presumptuous, is it?"

"No, but it's risky."

He smiled again. "It is daring, if you ask for it honestly. But then, you see, if you receive what you have honestly asked for, it is a gift and not a punishment."

"You make everything so simple."

"It is simple."

"There's no way out, with you!"

"I try to show you the way out."

"Yes. Yes." Frustrated, I stared at him glumly. "Have the birds gone, Father?" I said at last, out of despair. "The martins in your birdhouse? Have they left for South America?"

"Yes. On August second. All together. I awoke in the morning, and they were gone. You see," he continued, after an instant's pause, "they show us a sense of timing beyond human time. They have, as your sister might say, a *mystique* of time."

"God's order," I responded dully.

"Yes, certainly. For it has nothing to do with man's hours and minutes, does it? It is more urge, more movement," he spread his hands joyously, "the vast cosmic movement! So if we concede the birds obey this timing, we concede there is this timing. And if there is this timing, could it not move us, too, if we could only be still enough to hear it, if we could be simple enough to wait for it?"

I had been listening more to the music, the passion, of

his voice, than to the words. I sat up slowly, as if acquiring a second wind at the close of an ordeal. "What are you trying to tell me, Father?"

"That there is a time for you, too, for what you need, for what you ask, for whatever you must do."

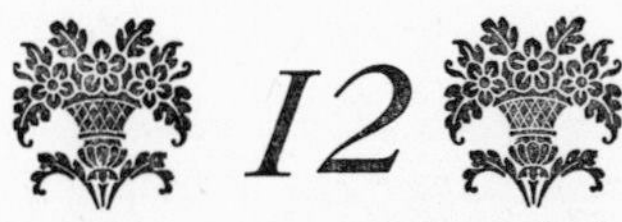

12

The party to end parties. Everything was in readiness. I lay on my chaise, before dressing, suspending desires and fears, perhaps as close to the will-lessness Father Bonneau had recommended as I could come. The house, the night, seemed to hold its breath. Perhaps the dragon was at last about to rouse himself; the darker sky in the afternoon wasn't promising. Downstairs, pyramids of flowers silently exhaled their daintily erotic fragrance, and winking glasses waited in ranks on snowy tables. The extra help, hired from the golf club, had retired to the back porch. I stirred the air with an old paper fan I had found in a drawer, which had "*Café de la Paix*" printed across it; souvenir, no doubt, of Mother's Paris honeymoon.

Bernice came to the door with what Branzini called my Bacchanalian dress, the white chiffon with green velvet grape leaves. At the last minute I changed my mind. "I can't wear it."

Bernice dropped her arms an inch or two as if to say, My God, what next? "It is all pressed, Madame."

"I can't wear it!" I told her. "I'm too thin for it now.

It's too elaborate. Most of my guests will be coming straight from the bazaar—"

She put on a face of phony deference; her eyes said, Why didn't you think of all this before? She went off to my wardrobe to find me a substitute.

Why indeed? How many happenings are imprisoned in my mind, some to break out inopportunely like this one, some never to emerge at all?

It was at the Tuscan villa. Midnight. Branzini and I had come home from a party, or perhaps one of our own had just ended. I was wearing the white chiffon dress. We went out to stand on the terrace for a few minutes. The moon was full, the sky blanched. Moon-shadows of cypress trees, black as ink, reached across the lawn below; the fountain, lifting narrow glittering tongues, prattled softly to itself in an unending soliloquy. Branzini, half-sitting on the balustrade, his eye sockets filled with darkness, commanded, "Go down there. Dance for me." It was a challenge: Tempt me.

I smiled, removing my sandals. It was a dream, I told myself, going down the steps. I would make it a dream, exempting the faintly sickening sense of the grotesque, obviating awkwardness. It was a myth, the old story of the nymph enticing the mortal, the nobleman worn smooth and impotent by the rub of civilized centuries. I would lose myself in my own spell.

I see myself now as if in one of those surrealist, avant-garde films, moving in and out of the moon-shadows, turning, slowly turning, limbs and draperies intertwining, hair swaying, falling over the blind, rapt face. . . . Was I graceless? Was it embarrassing? I see the dress float to the grass. I pity and admire: the pale body moves with unintentional innocence. . . .

But when I came to a halt at last, panting, laughing, my body shining with a fine dew of perspiration, my arms lifted to the terrace, there was no one there. "Carlo?" I called softly; perhaps he had moved down into the shadows. Then I heard his car start up on the other side of the house, and I listened to it fade away down the drive; he was off on one of his night-prowls, never explained. I might or might not find him the next morning, sleeping soundlessly, smiling, in his bed. . . . The breath left my body completely for a moment, the perspiration cooled. I turned my face to the small white face of the moon, my arms still upraised as if frozen, and a sigh, a laugh, a rattle, came from my throat. Charming, I made the small white face say to me, just as I had made the dance a dream. Lovely! Captivating!

I swung about and gathered up my dress. I was trembling, and an attack of vertigo blacked everything for an instant. Scarcely bothering to cover myself, I went up to my room, and there, cold, frail, naked, old as mythology itself, I crawled into my bed. . . .

Bernice returned to my sitting room with the sari, all gossamer, palest pink woven with gold. No special association leaped out of hiding to defile it, and I nodded. She bore it away to her pressing board, saying, "You have only a little while before you must dress."

I had been to the bazaar in the morning, before the heat of the day became oppressive. Kitty is actually chairman of the handwork booth, and forgetting my aversion to lady-chairmen, I set out to see her there, in charge, and erase my picture of the beleaguered Katherine bent over a washtub of bruised water lilies. It's as if I must cancel as many of Mother's legacies as possible. Do I hope in this way to cancel Mother's ghost, disarm it one by one of its weapons?

The bazaar sprawls over the old parade ground back of the Civil War monument. Towering elms filter down a lofty indeterminate shade. I arrived just ahead of the opening hour, and the women were still setting out their wares; only a few early customers wandered among the booths. I stood back for a few minutes and took in the attractive scene among the great tree trunks, the yellow tents, the scattered figures, the subdued mutter of voices in the morning quiet.

I watched Kitty before she knew I was there. She was stringing multicolored potholders on a line between the tentpoles, and when the other workers consulted her she gave directions over her shoulder. She seemed undistracted and unhurried, very young-womanly in her blue striped shirtwaist dress. Her face was serious, rather pale, but it was transformed suddenly as she laughed at something Margo said, and the smile lingered on her lips.

She might have been Katherine's grownup sister, Katherine's mother. And silently I informed my ghost, This is what your dying did for her. You have no hold on her any more, you can't have. On me, yes, I can't deny that, but not on her! You're wasting your time on her; you might as well leave her alone.

A number of red-headed children swarmed about at Ginny's bidding. They were unloading brightly painted bird houses from a truck backed up to the tent, and placing them on display. The youngest child, wearying, pressed his head against his mother's hip, and without pausing in her instructions Ginny clasped his head in her hand comfortingly. Four years old, he must be. How often does Rob—I found myself on the point of wondering, studying Ginny's full bosom and sturdy legs, and cut myself short, revolted by my wistful prurience, and indeed by Ginny's easy prerogative.

Kitty's face lit up with surprise and pleasure as I approached, and almost simultaneously a shadow fled across it, something close to fear, or dread, and then she welcomed me. Margo saluted gaily over the aprons, and eventually Ginny, unable to avoid me, squeezed out her stillborn, "Hi."

I gave Kitty a check. "There used to be a lot of rivalry between the booths, wasn't there?"

Kitty looked up from the check to my face. "Oh gosh, Althea."

"After all, it's for the hospital."

"Yes," she said faintly. Her gaze swept over the grounds as if she had almost forgotten that the purpose of the bazaar was to benefit the sick, almost forgotten her sorrows, her secrets. I felt a pang that I had reminded her, and then once again I was impatient with her: why couldn't she let go of them?

She brightened as if at my demand. "Look, girls," she cried, waving the check, "we're over the top already!"

I was hailed from other booths as I left. They were looking forward to the party, they said. They had always wanted to see Northwater, one of them told me, and then gulped, wondering if that was quite tactful, considering that its notoriety was based on tragedy. But I was pleased; I wanted them to see it. I wanted the doors and windows wide open and people swarming through it. . . .

The flower booth was greatly enlarged from Mother's day; they were selling vegetables, too, and men as well as women were at work. They were obviously enjoying themselves. Mother wouldn't have approved. I smiled.

Bernice brought a glass of champagne to my dressing table. "Just one," she urged. "To relax you." Perhaps it worked. My reflected eyes seemed enlarged; my face glowed with an extraordinary calm. And when Bernice had fastened the intricate clasps of the sari and I turned from the long mirror, she stood back and nodded slowly. She kept on nodding as if she couldn't think what to say.

I put out my hand to her. "Thank you, my faithful friend."

She seized my hand between both of hers, her eyes brimming. "I am glad they will see you like this," she said. She scurried away.

I took up a position under the wind chimes, and there was a last immobilized moment.

The Japanese lanterns glowed orange up and down the veranda and in the rose garden, inviting couples to wander; Clarence had remembered where Daddy used to place them. Bernice and Sarah, in starched uniforms, hovered within. The bartenders had taken up their stations, and waiters in the dining room stood guard over chafing dishes and molded salads and decorated hams. In the cleared, echoing arena of the hall, the piano sounded *A*, the fertile *A*, producing a cascade of notes from trumpet and saxophone, guitar and clarinet, and then lapsed into silence again.

It was then that I heard a dry pattering as if something ran lightly up over the lawns, encroaching on the house, and the wind chimes stirred and murmured. I drew the scarves of my gown about my arms. The gardens, the night, seemed suddenly filled with invisible motion, with mischievous watching. A congregation of the uninvited, perhaps—Mother, Daddy, and Kitty's Indians. . . .

A car door slammed, voices sounded in the driveway. The bartenders came to attention. The orchestra, at a signal from Bernice, struck up a bouncing melody. The first guests had arrived.

They came by two's and three's and then in droves, laughing, expectant, intrigued, flowing in a river to the momentary arrest of my hand and then on to the bar at the end of the veranda and the brilliant, pulsating hall and the dining room. Most of them had changed to party clothes. Kitty wore her long white dress with the velvet sash. "Shall I stay by you and help with the—" she began, but Simon swept her away to the music, and I had a glimpse of him launching her with great care and concentration into the melee.

"You look as if you'd floated out of the Taj Mahal," Margo told me in a swooning voice, and drifted on with a contingent from the handwork booth.

Jack remained behind to keep an eye on me; or rather, to keep me in the span of his quick-silver vision. He didn't look in the least concerned, smiling and leaning against a pillar, chatting with passing friends, but I knew it was concern that kept him there. And again I felt buoyed up by his guardianship, the quaint and delightful family-sense he gave me, and again I thought of Daddy, or rather, of the little girl in white fur holding Daddy's hand. . . .

The old phrases fell automatically from my lips: "How nice to see you. . . . How good of you to come. . . . How charming you look. . . ." I was playing the old role again, and Jack seemed to be enjoying the performance.

"Can I get you something to drink?" he asked, in a lull. "You sound a little dry. A glass of champagne?"

"No, thanks, I've had one. Champagne always used to make me a bit frisky."

"It's your night to frisk, isn't it?"

"Yes," I said soberly. "It is. So it is." The wind chimes tinkled loudly in a rush of air and we both heard the first mutter of thunder. "My God, Jack, it isn't going to rain, is it?"

There was a shout of laughter from the bar-end of the veranda, and the trumpets drove brass notes into the uproar. "At this point," Jack answered, raising his voice, "it won't make much difference!"

The Clays appeared before me, solemn of mien, Ginny still in her wraparound skirt and dusty moccasins. "We stayed to close the booth," she told me, her glance sweeping my costume as if it presented a reproach. "I thought Kate should be here with you."

And, "You're looking well," said Rob, taking my hand. His eyes moved quickly away from me; he, too, although in a different way, seemed surprised, disconcerted, by my appearance.

"You must both be tired," I told them soothingly, setting myself to be gracious in inverse ratio to a mounting impulse to be rude. Whether due to the champagne Bernice had given me, or Jack's encouragement, or the heaviness, the dull discontent I indignantly sensed in this couple, almost as if they in turn presented a reproach to me, I was in danger, I knew, of doing or saying something unforgivable. Bubbles of laughter seemed to rise from my vacuum of will-lessness.

"Well, at least *he* hasn't been on his feet all day," Ginny responded, slipping a proprietary arm through his, and their arms remained crossed like the wooden ones of window dummies.

"You have been working *for* the hospital," I reminded her in a murmur, "and he has been working *in* it."

Touché, her flat smile told me. She rubbed her jaw

against Rob's sleeve. She always had her trump card handy. "But *he* doesn't have seven children to cope with."

Oh patronizing bitch, I all but sang in return. And I realized heartbrokenly that I loved Rob the least when he stood silently by like this, allowing himself to be minimized in the third person. I wanted to knock their heads together. I wanted to seize Ginny by the forearms and shake her, telling her, He is good, he is yours, his youth is withering for love, forget your insufficient self-image and your envy and give this man comfort!

And where was my pity, my sense of mercy? I seemed to have lost then whatever it was that held this couple inviolate.

"Rob, darling," I said, hanging on to self-restraint for dear life, "do take her over to the bar for a drink, and then get her some food. Perhaps that will refresh her."

It was the third person applied to herself, I think, and not the word of endearment, which brought forward Ginny's jaw, and another glimpse in her eyes of that pathetic, self-accusing astonishment.

"You haven't danced with me yet." Jack's fingers touched my elbow. I grinned at him, turning away from the Clays, and Jack grinned back. Thunder sounded again, the first explosion multiplying itself, spilling across the floor of the night. There was no doubt about it; the dragon had got to its feet. We moved to the hall, and the light, the music, sucked us in.

"Oh lord, Jack, thank you. I was about to disgrace myself."

He clasped me lightly. He was a nice dancer, with an easy timing. He said, "There isn't anything that girl wouldn't do for you if you were in trouble."

"I'm sure of it," I answered. "But that's the kind of magnanimity I don't admire; you have to be in trouble first."

"What kind do you admire?"

"The kind all of you show her. Loving the unlovable."

"People are funny," he advised drily.

"I agree."

"I mean," he added, "we're all people."

"Yes. I've been unlovable, too."

"I thought you were the spoiled one."

"I was. It seems to have the same effect as being unloved. Kitty knew her own worth better than I did."

Kitty whirled by, then, her pearly face lifted, her skirt belling out behind her; she was cut in on again and again but she didn't smile. "I only wish I could set her free of this place. I thought this party might take some of the curse off it."

"I tried to tell you: you can't do everything for her."

"Jack, what *can* I do? What can I do?"

I wonder what he would have answered. Simon cut in then, and Jack merely smiled, and moved away toward Kitty.

"I have long yearned," said Simon, like the courtly buffoon in a Restoration comedy, "to hold you in my arms!"

His voice dropped to normal, and hastily, with some shyness, he stated over the top of my head, "You are quite exquisite tonight, my dear," and then he executed a pirouette with his long legs that all but lifted me off the floor.

The bulb-tipped antlers, the horned sconces, the chandeliers radiated light. Glass eyes glittered, swords and helmets and the sweeping pipes of the organ gleamed; even the music was sun-colored. Faces in the churning mass were like masks, self-forgetful, ecstatic. . . . Voices called to me in passing: "What a ball, Althea . . . what a fantastic house. . . ."

Is it gay, Daddy, I asked silently; would you think it really gay? But not even Daddy had given a party as grand as this, and Northwater, marvelous in its hideousness, comical in its perfectly preserved solemnity, had never lent itself so handsomely to pleasure. Had it come into its own? Had the spell been broken?

The vacuum within me gave way then. Or perhaps the inevitable exhaustion had caught up with me. Rob cut in, his hand took mine, his arm moved to clasp me. But we came to a halt and for an instant I leaned my forehead against his cheek. "I must stop. I must get out of here." Without a word, as if he had expected this at least, he guided me out to the veranda.

Another rush of cooling air met us, and lightning throbbed briefly. The crowd at the bar, with Ginny, flushed and vociferous, in the middle of it, obliviously continued its hubbub. Would Rob go to her rescue?

"I'll leave you here," I told him, and a forsaking despair must have touched my voice, for I was thinking, Follow me if you want to, stay if you want to, there isn't anything I can't accept from you now. "I'm going down to the boathouse," I told him. "I've had enough for a while."

"No," he began, "please don't—"

But we had reached the other end of the veranda and I slipped away into the glimmering darkness, running down over the lawn. A drop of rain fell like a blessing on the center of my brow, and the air was sweet, but the vacuum had given way to anguish and a voice crying, Love, love, love, with each footfall, and I thought, I must die, I must die. . . .

He caught up with me at the foot of the lawn. "Althea, wait—!"

I turned and took his hand. We continued to the boathouse together, and without a word of consent we went up the outside staircase, lighted convulsively by the oncoming storm, and into the old playroom.

For an instant, on the threshold, I couldn't move. The preserved heat of the summer, the smell of mice, varnished wood, canvas, old games, old passions, were overpowering. I fell back a little, and Rob's steadying hand left mine and gripped my arm.

Then, tentatively I stepped forward, and crossed the room to draw down the tops of the front windows, and Rob followed to assist me, and we stood, each in his own window, arms crossed on the lowered sashes, the rain-scent pouring past our faces, the scarves of my gown flowing out behind me—listening to the sigh of the deluge advancing across the lake, waiting. . . .

And once again the movement of air and water washed away distress, divested us of all that weighed on us, purified us.

I wasn't going to do anything desperate, I wanted to reassure him; but he knew that, in our present surrender. I needed mercy, I had to find it again with you. You must be comforted. We both must be comforted, for I have nothing but the present. . . .

I didn't need to say it.

Music and sounds of revelry came faintly from the house. Would someone dance with the bear, would the organ come groaning to life? I forgave Daddy then, I smiled on him. All of my life, my loneliness, was distilled into this moment.

The storm broke in full force, the rain swept up from the lake and fell with a crash on the roof of the boathouse, the sky opened in white light.

We turned to each other. Rob put out his hand, saying, "Come here to me," as though he intended to put a protective arm about me, but instead, still without will, we closed together softly, and starvation, tenderness, anguish, engulfed us. We moved presently to one of the divans and helplessly we surrendered even our separateness, the white light consuming us, and all of it, in some poignant, purifying way, obliterating past and future and at last even present, was mercy.

Zebstrow, the notebook is nearly finished. I am tempted to will it to you, in answer to the questions I couldn't answer to your face, and to let you know I did learn to think. I am about to take the last turning; Father Bonneau, of course, gave me the necessary push. Kitty will arrive soon. I'm not afraid. The hour in the boathouse last night left me with few desires of my own. I want only to give her peace. Just as her mysteries are my mysteries, so her peace is my peace.

I slept a short while this morning, after the sun rose, and then I went to see Father Bonneau. I had telephoned ahead, and his rambunctious housekeeper conducted me to his study at a restrained gallop. She must spend all her time relentlessly scrubbing and polishing; the windows, floors, woodwork look sterilized, and Father Bonneau has retreated to a last stronghold at the back of the house, his own little island of untidiness. In an immaculate room with a green carpet and glittering glass-fronted bookcases, his desk is a friendly jumble; papers and books drift about an old standard typewriter, and I noted lurking amongst them a box of tacks, keys, pruning clippers, spectacles, pipe tobacco, an empty cup and saucer, and one very small red sneaker.

He rose and shook hands and wafted me, so to speak, into a grandfatherly leather armchair, and while he chatted and shifted the clutter in search of his pipe, I studied him anew in his own surroundings. The little lost sneaker had been placed on a pile of books as some people display a bronze bust. A sprig of berries leaned from a water glass. I thought how all delightful things are attracted to him and cling to him, and some invisible armor or indifference causes all ugliness to fall away from him. I thought how lightly, how tenderly, he wears the burden of mortality.

He unearthed his pipe and filled it, and then, having gone to all that trouble, set it aside and sat back in his swivel chair and smiled at me, and I said, "Father, I came to see you on a matter of business."

"Yes," he agreed attentively, clasping his hands over his vest.

I considered for a moment, my eyes fastened on the stray sneaker. "I would like to leave Northwater to your church."

"That is very generous of you." Did nothing ever surprise him?

"I had thought it would make a good retreat house, something like that, but now I think it would be better as a place where—where children, orphans—" My voice, suddenly blocked by inexplicable tears, ground to a stop.

I cleared my throat and began again. "Perhaps some order of nuns might use it in summer for children."

"It would make a happy place for them, wouldn't it?"

"I hope so. And I know my sister would be relieved not to have to inherit it; dismantle it and sell it. . . ."

"Of course."

I broke off. "There is so much you understand!"

He smiled. "There is so much I do not understand."

"And that doesn't trouble you?"

"On the contrary, it is what makes life so entrancing."

"Yes. Entrancing." I frowned, not wishing to give way again, and trying to concentrate on the matter at hand. "I would appreciate your advising me, Father, as to how to instruct my lawyer."

"Now?"

"Yes, now. I think it must be done as quickly as possible."

"Very well." His mind works simply and clearly, for all the disorder of his desk. He found pen and paper, wrote down names and addresses, and in short order I had the information I needed.

I sat back in the leather chair and a long unexpected sigh came from me. Father Bonneau waited with his hands folded, as if we were travelers thrown together on a long journey and had all the time in the world to converse.

"This is not atonement, Father."

"Oh no, I didn't suppose it to be."

"I wouldn't let myself off that easily."

"I know you would not."

"You know that, too!" I had been feeling almost giddy, with the burden of Northwater lifted, like a culpable child rejoicing in a momentary reprieve. But Father Bonneau's expression sobered me; his compassion encompassed not only what he knew of me but also what he did not know.

He asked, "Do you still feel you need to make a confession?"

"Yes, I still need to."

He was silent an instant, and then he spoke out quietly, "Do you wish to make it to me? Now?"

My nails dug into the seams of the leather chair. I looked beyond his head through an open window. I could see the deserted martin house over the grape arbor, and the steam and sparkle of the wet garden drying in the sun. It was very quiet; only the crickets throbbed tremulously. "I can't make it to you, Father! I don't wish to transfer my sins to you! It would be too easy, and it would not absolve me."

He shook his head. "What a puritan you are."

I had to laugh. "Puritan, Father!"

"We Catholics are not so hard on ourselves."

"I never thought of you as lenient."

"We are not lenient; we are practical. Now listen to me." His invincibility shone out all over his face and figure, bringing me bolt upright, reminding me that the gentle grace of this man generated its own power. He said, "If I in my own heart can forgive your sins, however monstrous, without knowing them, do you not believe God can forgive them, knowing them, loving you better than you love yourself? Do you fear Him so much, or do you underestimate Him, or do you try to do both at once?"

He didn't give me time to answer. "You believe in love, you can love, it shows in your face. Do you not see that love is also forgiveness? How do you dare exclude yourself from this forgiveness? You do not have to confess to me. You do not have to seek absolution. But you must not take it upon yourself to withhold from yourself the love that has already been given you and the forgiveness that already belongs to you!"

I bowed my head in my hands, my fingers just short of my ears. *Love, forgiveness, love, forgiveness. . . .* The words made a kind of humming lullaby, a pellucid atmosphere about my exhausted brain, just as air and water had given me mercy. "Yes," I said, looking up. "All right. It's time." I began to get to my feet.

"And what does that mean?"

"God's timing! You told me: there would be a time for what I need and what I must do. It concerns my sister; something troubles her deeply and I can't let her go on bearing it in silence. I've been afraid of her. I think I've always been afraid of her, as she was of me, yet differently: she was my conscience. Well, my fear seems to have gone away. All fear. Perhaps it's a result of disposing of Northwater, or perhaps I've absorbed some of your love and forgiveness, enough to offer them and ask for them." My fingers touched the small red sneaker. "Father, may I come back to you?" He was standing also, his hands loosely clasped behind his back.

"Not necessarily for absolution," I explained, "but for some little formality, so that I can tell you, at least, that I've done all I could do. Or if I'm not well enough, will you come to me?"

"I will come to you."

"You know what I'm asking, Father?" I couldn't quite meet his eyes. I couldn't bring myself to utter the Gothic word *deathbed.* "I would be grateful if you would be there."

"Yes," he said. And this simple consent promised such a brilliant, exhilarating auspice, so utterly reassuring, that I smiled, realizing I almost looked forward to the event. "I will be there," he said.

I stopped in Judge Philbody's office over the bank building. He is one of an earlier breed of New England gentlemen—eccentric, unhurried, courteous, a little fierce. It may be that Simon Goodfellow will carry on the tradition. Judge Philbody knew my mother and we had to go over old ground at a gracious tempo. At last we cleared up the amenities and got down to the business of my will and Northwater. I think he wondered at first if I were of sound mind. In his sedate office my intention, spearheaded by the word Catholic, sounded almost unlawful. He was thinking, no doubt, of my mother's feelings. But he respected my determination; that he could admire. A dry smile puckered his polished Yankee face. "Very well," he said. "So be it. I will see to the matter at once."

It was done. Northwater's future was ordained, and I was all but free of it. I hoped Kitty would feel as I did.

Rob's mileage-worn sports car was in my driveway when I returned. The blood surged out in my veins like an involuntary cry: my love! I had thought he would stay away for a day or two, to recover his ethics, his detachment from me, and I wanted him to if he needed to. And again I marveled, that I could love a man in this way, without demands or expectations. I marveled at the joy in it, the freedom from bitterness, the newness, the feeling, still, of innocence.

He was waiting in the screened-in enclosure of the veranda, standing at the railing, his arms folded over his chest. The sodden lanterns had been taken down, the glasses removed, the cigarette butts swept away; the gala night of merrymaking and celestial fireworks had revolved into the past, expunged by the calm of morning.

How shining-haired he was, how muscular, how much more vulnerable than Father Bonneau! He heard my footsteps and, turning, watched me approach without changing expression. He was a man with responsibilities again, loyalties, self-respect. Perhaps after last night he had rededicated himself. It wasn't that he seemed happier, or less so; but the look of tragic, premature age was gone.

I closed the screen door behind me and said, "Hello, Rob," quietly.

He moved to reach for my hand. He didn't speak for a moment, looking at me gravely, as if there were much that was understood between us, without words. His handclasp was firm, unrepentant. "The party took its toll from you, didn't it?"

"That was to be expected." An unusual flush crept about my eyes. "It was worth it."

He nodded, again as if there were no need to utter agreement. He indicated a chair for me and we sat down, our knees almost touching, and he said lightly, "We might as well get this over with," and took the thermometer from his breast pocket, shook it down and inserted it in my mouth, and crouching forward, pressed his fingers to my wrist.

There is always something moving, to me, in this procedure, this simple communion, he counting and I submissively being counted; we aren't man and woman then, or even the well and the sick, but common humanity. I am humbled; he is charity. We are one in human frailty.

He sat back again, glanced at the thermometer, pocketed it, studied me.

"I'm running a temperature," I guessed aloud, reading his face. "I'm not surprised." I took a little breath. "In fact, I have a feeling I'm on the verge of another attack, Rob, and that it may be the last one."

His eyes were at once bluer, darker, but he didn't demur. He took my hand once more. "I would like you to go into the hospital right now."

"Not right now, Rob. I'm expecting Kitty this afternoon. There is something I must settle with her."

He ran his fingers over the bones in the back of my hand. He said, "I love you very much, Althea."

"I love you, Rob."

He looked up. "It doesn't have too much to do with last night. It isn't something I feel because of that."

"No. I know."

"Although I can't touch you like this without wanting you."

"Are you sorry?"

"I just don't want to add to your—to the things that already trouble your conscience."

"And yours, Rob? Your conscience doesn't trouble you?"

"That's the surprising thing." Thoughtfully he closed my hand in his. "I feel as if everyone I know, and will know, everyone I come in contact with, or treat, will benefit from what I feel for you. Can you understand that?"

"Yes."

"I had some pretty rigid principles. I must have been pretty inflexible. I practiced a kind of academic morality rather than love." His grasp on my hand tightened. "Althea, last night was like discovering, like penetrating, the very heart of life, like looking into the furnace of the earth. I didn't know I was capable of a surrender like that, to another person, to you, I didn't know it was possible to give one's self so—" He couldn't find the adverb and shook his head. "Althea, this morning I loved even my own children better."

I shut my eyes. A gratitude, a sadness, overwhelmed

me, and I felt like one of his children, and the mother of his children. I said, finally, "And Ginny?"

"Yes, Ginny, too. For years I must have kept her—everyone—at arm's length. It's as if your mercy had entered in, where I didn't know there was a need for mercy. I don't know what will come of it, but she feels the difference, and she's quieter, less defensive. Oh lord, I can't say it properly, I'm not even sure yet what I'm trying to say—"

"Well, I think I know."

"Yes, I think you do." He studied me, his eyes heavy, lingering. "It will be a long time before I realize just what you are in my life. Even *grande passion* sounds insignificant. I will have known you such a short time and it will have made such a difference."

We were silent. I knew, not without tenderness, that the shortness of time made his love all the deeper, made it in a sense feasible, eliminating future complications, canceling our age difference. Perhaps he knew this, too, with the same tenderness. Our eyes clung together for a long time, our hands. He sat back. "Now." He drew me to my feet. "I want you to let me make arrangements for you to go into the hospital tonight."

My gaze moved from his face to the garden drowsing in the noon sun, the roof of the boathouse, the shimmering water, as if in farewell. How beautiful it was! But I felt no regret, no nostalgia. The part it had played in my life had all but ended, as if I had already taken leave of it. I turned to Rob again. "Yes. All right. Tonight."

He made a sound then, of protest, of anguish, of acceptance, drawing me into his arms, and we held each other close for a moment.

He released me. "I'll come for you after office hours. It may be late, but don't worry. I'll come."

I waited for Kitty in the library, neutral ground, with no little pink clock ticking, no accoutrements of my own domain. I had lighted the fire to relieve the gloom, and the sun had traveled around to the west to glow in the stained glass tops of the windows and cast glints of ruby and cobalt and emerald about the room.

She knew this was to be a showdown. She entered so silently, her head bowed, like someone deep in forethought, and then she looked up and smiled at me faintly, hopefully. I offered her the big leather chair opposite me, near the fire, and as if she were cold she curled in it tensely and tucked her skirt about her sandaled feet. Her face was smooth and pale as marble, unrevealing, wary.

I had no plan. I had only calm and the extraordinary absence of fear. Everything that was to be said was still a blank. I trusted to Father Bonneau's timing.

I told Kitty what I had arranged to do about Northwater.

"Oh, Althea, you didn't!"

"You don't like the idea?"

"I think it's the most marvelous idea I ever heard of. *Oh*, you don't know what a relief this is!" She was almost laughing.

"I hoped you'd be glad."

"This terrible house, filled with children! It won't be

a monstrosity any more, or a joke, or haunted. Nothing else could have done it but children. How ever did you think of such a thing?"

"I have flashes of brilliance these days." I smiled. "No, it only came to me this morning in Father Bonneau's study. He didn't suggest it, of course, but he—his influence—is responsible."

"Yes. He's like one of the little saints, isn't he? I'm glad he is your friend."

"I am, too."

"Can you talk to him freely?"

Ah, now we were circling the main matter, coming closer. "Yes, I can talk to him."

"I mean, anything you need to say to someone, you can say to him?" She was studying the folds of her skirt, her bowed face shadowed by the firelight, dark crescents under her lowered lids.

"No, not anything. Not everything," I added, "I hope he can become your friend, too."

She didn't answer that. She smoothed the material of her skirt and suddenly looked up and gazed about her, her eyes unfocused, slightly protruding. "What do you think Mother would feel about it? About willing Northwater to a Catholic orphanage?"

So we had retreated again. "Do you need to ask? She'd be outraged."

"Maybe she wouldn't be." And without explaining the remark she posed another question: "Do you think she loved children at all?" She was still not looking at me, and we were both waiting, hovering, as it were, about the edge of the abyss.

"She loved you."

Kitty turned then to stare at me. "What did you say?"

"She loved *you.*"

"You say that as if I were the child she loved."

"You were."

She uncurled her legs and pressed her feet to the floor, her hands gripping the cushion of the chair on either side of her thighs. A faint sheen of perspiration gleamed now on her pale lids and upper lip. "Althea, I don't understand." She studied the floor as if she were trying to think it through for herself.

"You were the one she loved, Kitty. I must always have known that. You were the one she tried not to love. You were what Daddy left of himself in her. You looked like him, you were his virtues. Why else would she have had to enslave you? Why else would she have gone mad when you wanted to leave her?"

Slowly Kitty lifted haggard eyes to me. "And you, Althea?"

"Oh, Kitty, think! I was the one *he* loved. She made a whore of me, she exploited me, she encouraged me to offend. I was her revenge! I know, it sounds farfetched, but maybe it's not farfetched enough. I have a feeling Dr. Zebstrow would applaud. I only know this, Kitty: what she felt for me couldn't have been love, and what she felt for you could have been."

Now Kitty got stiffly to her feet, slowly crossed the

room to the windows facing the lake, and half-knelt on the leather cushion of the window seat. The late sunlight silhouetted her and I couldn't see her face. The room was very still. She was going to say it now, or I was, it didn't make much difference.

When Jack appeared in the doorway at that moment I could only look at him vacantly. Perhaps my face held him silent. He stayed where he was, immobilized by the crisis he intuitively sensed he had come upon.

"You killed her, didn't you?"

I felt myself disintegrating then, as if parts of me were separating, vanishing. My forehead seemed to lift and my brain to float away. No eyes, no ears. A throat without air.

We had broken into the sealed chamber.

"Yes," I said at last, answering Kitty. At last. "I killed her."

The parts were floating together again, connecting. My brain settled dizzily, a little askew. I breathed again. A chill passed over my quivering body, and the blood moved. "Kitty, Jack is here, too. I asked him to come."

She turned, not surprised.

He spoke to her, "Would you rather I go?"

I broke in, "No, please stay! Kitty, he heard. I wanted him to hear."

She nodded slowly; her thoughts were obviously still absorbed in this denouement, and his presence must have seemed normal in the midst of the abnormal. He stayed in the doorway, his face oddly elongated. The fire sighed, the only voice, for a few moments, in the room.

"How long, Kitty," I asked, "have you known?"

She answered in a murmur but quite steadily, "Since you wanted me to know." She had turned to the windows again. "You wanted me to stop blaming myself for her suicide, her apparent suicide. I realized you had come back to Northwater to set something right. I hoped you could tell Father Bonneau, because I saw how it weighed on you, and I knew if you couldn't tell him you would have to tell me. I couldn't let you go on sparing me. I was afraid you'd never be able to tell anyone—!"

"Yes," I said, "it's been a greater burden for you, because you were carrying it for me, and I've watched it grow heavier and heavier." I got unsteadily to my feet and Jack leaped to put a hand under my elbow, and then he stayed beside me, his arm around my shoulder.

"It's all right, Althea," he said, gently and helplessly. "It's all right."

I stared at him, somewhat shocked. Was he compromising his principles out of family loyalty? But it wasn't time to accept comfort. I moved to the desk that centered the room, with its lighted Tiffany lamp, and supporting myself against it, I leaned toward my sister.

"Kitty, she never knew, she never saw me. She was crying hysterically with her head in her arms. I didn't even know if the revolver was loaded until it went off. I held it in the handkerchief she kept it wrapped in, in her bedside table, and after it went off I slipped it into her hand and closed her fingers—"

"Althea," Kitty whirled about to me, "you don't have to tell me this!"

"Yes, I have to. You have to know it. Jack has to know it. You kept trying to tell me she murdered herself; she had attempted suicide, she would attempt it again, she threatened to kill you. That was meant to exonerate me, wasn't it? Kitty, there is no exoneration for me except in confession to you. I couldn't tell Father Bonneau because it was you I had to tell." I hesitated a moment. "And I have to tell you this, too: even though it's been horror to me, the greatest horror, so great that it's been blocked away in my mind all these years, even though I couldn't live with myself sanely because I killed her, I've never been sorry she died." My hands gripped the edge of the desk. "In a sense she did murder herself."

Kitty cried out, "You killed her for me!"

"Oh, no, Kitty, I can't let you believe that. Jack," I said, turning, "she must never believe that!" His back to the fire, he frowned at me through his own thoughts. "Kitty, I'd hated her for so long! Yes, I hated what she did to you, and the threat I heard her make was the last straw, but I killed her for what she did to me, too, and to Daddy. I don't know what would have happened if the circumstances hadn't been exactly right that afternoon, if I hadn't been in my sitting room and heard your quarrel. I might never have done it. The idea had never occurred to me before, not consciously. We might have gone on living together forever, trapped, the three of us; my God, what a ghastly thought! But the circumstances *were* right, and she threatened you so irrevocably, and I did it without thinking twice."

"You've suffered more than I ever did," Kitty said,

almost angrily, her eyes flashing with tears. "Althea, I can't bear it! Because now that you're dying you've become a person who could be happy." Her eyes appealed to Jack, and he quickly crossed the room to her.

I smiled. "I've become a person who could be happy because I'm dying." I stepped around the desk to the window seat where they stood, and sat down, and Kitty sat down beside me. "It's only important that *you* be happy," I told her. "This has done awful things to you, this summer."

She reached up, without looking behind her, for Jack's hand, and clasped it to her shoulder. "Maybe it hasn't done awful things at all."

"It hasn't." Jack seated himself just behind Kitty, leaning forward and a little sideways with an elbow in the window sill. "True, it hasn't been what you might call happy, but it's done something good for us."

Kitty's eyes shone on me in an imperative way, insisting I accept what she believed. "Althea, I don't feel guilty any more. Something that's been knotted up inside me all these years has come unknotted. No wonder I couldn't get pregnant. I'm at peace." Her hand tightened on Jack's. "He's right, something good has happened this summer. We saw it happening in your face, and we felt it happening in ourselves. Do you know how beautiful you've become? You've made us think; you've made us—open our eyes. We none of us have so terribly much time, do we? I don't care what you've done in the past. It's been erased, or at least balanced, by what you've made us feel, by this—this—"

I smiled again. "Love and forgiveness?"

"Yes!" she exclaimed softly. "Yes. Love and forgiveness. What lovely words. That's it exactly." Her free hand reached for mine, gripping it firmly. "Do you know the saying, that we are all the people we've ever known? We are something of you now, Althea, something more than we were, we'll always be, all of us who have known you."

I shut my eyes. Perhaps I had already begun to exist in them. I felt drained of myself, my old self, my new self.

Jack got to his feet. "Come on, Kate," he told her quietly. "I don't think we need to say anything more. Althea's had it. We've all had it, for one day. Let's go home." He bent over me and cupped my face in his hands. "Will you come with us?" It was more command than plea.

But I wanted these last few hours to myself. "Thank you, Jack. I'd rather stay here."

A hint of amusement and irony flickered in his eyes; he knew at once it was no use trying to persuade me. "All right, then." He bent and kissed me lightly on the lips. "You rest now," he said.

I'm waiting for Rob. Bernice has packed a bag for me. The house is very still. The old vibrations of hate and terror have spent themselves and dispersed; the atmosphere is flat, like that of an empty house between tenants. Only the little pink clock in its pink leather cathedral makes its tiny hurrying sound. And even though I burn with fever, I am at home within myself.

Another hallucination; perhaps the last. Mother appeared again, pausing in my sitting-room door as if she were going down the hall from her own room to the stairs. She didn't speak.

"Are you satisfied?" I whispered.

She gave no sign, standing there tall and proud.

"Have you pardoned me?"

Still she refused to answer, and I saw her as she must have been in reality—obstinate, mistaken, childish, driven, unwitting—and I pitied her for the first time as Kitty has done all along. I told her, "I pardon *you.*"

Her eyes rounded foolishly, and then she tipped back her head and laughed in silence, and clasping her hands against her lips for an instant as if to hold back sound, she finished by blowing me a kiss, of release, of derision, of defiance, and still laughing, she went away down the hall.

I am close to the ultimate answer, the infinite explanation I have glimpsed before. I used to think of it as total darkness, but the irresistible Father Bonneau has convinced me it is at least possible to think of it as total light. I tremble, not with fear but with wonder. Something in me wants to cry, but I am smiling. I can't stop smiling.

I, too, am at peace.